WHERE IS MY SISTER?

Kathleen Shields

PublishAmerica
Baltimore

First printing

ISBN: 1-4137-4856-2
PUBLISHED BY PUBLISHAMERICA, LLLP
www.publishamerica.com
Baltimore

Printed in the United States of America

DEDICATION

I dedicate this book to my sister, Kim. She has the strength, courage, integrity, love, and sense of humor that carries a woman through the toughest of times with a smile on her face.

PROLOGUE

It's not uncommon to be approached by one of the pleasantly confused residents who oftentimes mistake you for their loved one. Here at Oak Creek Retirement Home there is one resident who tugs at your heartstrings. Her name is Frannie. She retains her natural beauty, easily visible beneath the lines of time that crisscross her delicate face. Her soft brown eyes are lovely with long gray lashes. They see clearly, but if you look deeply into those daunting eyes, you will see that she is confused. She has been here for over twelve years, sharing a room with her older sister, Reeny. Recently Reeny moved to a nursing home. Frannie's short-term memory has begun the downward spiral caused by Alzheimer's disease. Her long-term memory is perfect. It is the recent daily and hourly memories that slip so suddenly from her grasp. Frannie is constantly asking staff and visitors, "Where is my sister? Reeny was in our room this morning and now she is gone. Reeny is lost. Please come with me. We must search for her. Where is my sister?" Staff, after being summoned by bewildered visitors or other residents, explain to Frannie that Reeny has moved to a nursing home. Frannie accepts this explanation and asks if someone will be taking her to see Reeny. The staff reminds Frannie her grandnephew, Ben, is coming this weekend and he will take her to see Reeny. As she shuffles back to her solitary room, she passes the activities room. Her attention is drawn to a tall, thin man who is very good looking for his age. There is something familiar about him. Frannie goes into the room and watches him. She cannot remember where she has seen him before. She sits down on the sofa next to him. He leans towards her and says in his soft voice, "Hi, Frannie, remember me? I'm your old boyfriend Tim Slocum. We've gotten to be good friends again here at Oak Creek Home." Tim's memory, like Frannie's, is being stolen by the thief of Alzheimer's disease. For now, they can each remember their young life together and share their joy of reminiscing. As she sits quietly next to Tim watching the elderly residents play games, read or knit, she sinks quietly into the past. Perhaps Tim can help her find Reeny. Her memory is vivid through the kaleidoscope of her younger years. She cannot remember who Tim is each day when she sees him. It is only when she reverts to the long ago days of her youth that she remembers Tim. She also remembers Reeny and Tom and Laurie and Ben. Slowly, she remembers where Tim fits into her life. She remembers that Tim does not know many things about her life. He does not know about important events, like Laurie's birth. She has secrets in her life that Tim does not know about. Her secrets would affect him deeply, if she were to tell him about them now. Her memory of long ago is sharp and clear. Groping desperately, she wonders if perhaps her memory of what happened fifty years ago can help her find Reeny. She thinks, *Ben is coming soon. Tim is here. These two things I remember, at least for a little while. I will talk to them both when Ben gets here. I will tell them the story of Reeny and me. I will tell them what happened with the baby after Tom died in the war and Tim went away to Northwestern. If I tell them my story, they will help me find Reeny. They will answer me when I ask, "Where is my sister?"*

CHAPTER 1

The decade of 1920 was considered enlightened, yet contraception was still a mystery to many young women. Most married couples ended up with more children than they could afford. The McFadden family was different. Stella McFadden suffered three miscarriages before delivering her daughter, Irene, affectionately called Reeny, safely into this world amid the razzle-dazzle of the roaring twenties. Reeny's birth made these parents joyous. Stan and Stella hoped for large, noisy family full of children. By the time Reeny was six years old they had given up this hope and settled into a calm routine with their only child. Their lives were quite content when they were blessed with the unexpected but welcome arrival of a second daughter they named Frannie.

The McFadden sisters were six years apart in age but grew up close together in a loving family atmosphere. A family having only two children was unusual, but the sisters felt complete with each other. Reeny was an Irish beauty. Her wavy auburn hair was highlighted with natural blonde streaks. The emerald green color of her large eyes caused people to stare into them, noticing the beautiful color and thick black lashes. Frannie was a contrast to Reeny. She was not beautiful, like Reeny, but she was very pretty. Frannie had silvery blonde hair, fair skin, and large dark brown eyes. Their age difference was significant and they looked nothing alike, yet two sisters could not have been closer. They complimented each other. They were popular with their friends, being very pretty and easy to talk to, but preferred their own company. As the sisters grew up, most of their time was spent together. Frannie adored her older sister. Each evening, as she sat atop her white eyelet bedspread on her twin bed and watched her older sister brush her long auburn hair, she would gaze at Reeny's delicate face and her heart would swell with pride as she said, "Reeny, I love you so much. We'll always be together, you and me." Her words were prophetic, more so than she could imagine in her young mind.

At the end of the 1920s, the crash of the volatile stock market caused the country to switch from knee-knocking, hand-clapping Charleston dancing couples, to middle-aged men jumping out windows to certain death rather than face financial ruin. Women stood in soup lines, their children with them, trying to endure the changes so abruptly taking place. The glitz and rattle of the roaring '20s gave way to the gloom and doom of Black Tuesday and its aftermath. Young men turned into bankrupt husbands and fathers, aged before their time. Faced with financial ruin, many of these men chose to end their lives rather than face the instantaneous destruction of their life's work. They left behind destitute, unprepared wives struggling to survive in a world where they had been taken care of by fathers, brothers, husbands and sons. The workforce had previously been off limits to this gentler sex. Now they were thrust to the forefront to provide for the children left behind by the men who could not face this time of economic disaster and shame. Every commodity was precious. Nothing was wasted. Although unemployment was rampant, everyone worked in some way. Paying jobs were scarce. Men, women, and children labored and sweated at whatever chore would bring dollars or food. If there was no work, backs were stretched over garbage cans or harvested fields, scourging for any scrap of food.

The stock market crash of 1929 caused hardship across America. It also gave backbone and generosity to the American people. Families were uprooted from homes and a great migration occurred throughout the country, as America tried to find a way out of destitution. The decade of the 1930s was a time of hardship for many Americans. This decade saw streams of families moving from the dust bowl of Oklahoma to the orchards of California. As Frannie entered her teen years, her sister, Reeny, was leaving hers. Mom and Dad referred to Reeny as their grown-up girl. As Reeny grew up, so did they all, in a very big hurry. The destitution seen at the beginning of the 1930s gave way to moving families resettling throughout the country. As the American people settled down in new homes and found new jobs, they could begin to think beyond their basic survival needs. By the time the next decade dawned, the American people became aware of the horrors of the war in Europe.

The calm of Frannie's childhood was swept away, replaced with patriot flag flying, marching bands, and parades of handsome, young men, off to foreign lands to protect the American democracy. Amidst a world at war, Frannie entered high school. In her small Midwestern hometown of Oak Creek, thousands of miles away from the front lines, Frannie was not immune to the sadness and tragedy the war wreaked upon a generation of young fighting soldiers and their loving, stalwart parents. Frannie's girlfriends had older brothers fighting the war in faraway places. There were too many times one of them would come to school with red, swollen eyes. Or there were the times when they would not come to school at all, absent for days. This little town grew quiet, somber citizens going about their daily business, always with the radio tuned to the latest news. It was a sad time when hometown boys in the military were listed as missing or dead in the war that raged in Europe.

Reeny's beau, Tom, was attending State University while Reeny worked as a secretary in a local law firm. One weekend each month, Tom would ride the Greyhound bus down from school to see Reeny. Reeny and Frannie would both put on stylish skirts with matching angora sweaters and walk down to Woolworth's to meet Tom's bus. Frannie was always full of questions on that walk. "Reeny, do you love Tom? How does it feel when he kisses you? Are his lips soft, and do you get butterflies in your stomach? Are you going to marry Tom?" and the questions went on and on. Reeny always answered Frannie truthfully. She loved Tom. His kisses tasted sweet, his lips were soft, her stomach tingled, and she floated away on a cloud when they were close together. She would talk seriously about wanting to marry Tom. She said he needed to finish college, yet she was afraid the war would soon interfere with Tom's education. With the threat of war looming over them both, there was urgency in their time together. Tom came down more often to visit Reeny. Frannie didn't go with her to meet him anymore. Their time together became precious.

One night Frannie lay awake, watching the clouds pass by the moon, sending shadows across the bedroom floor. Reeny came in, crying softly. Frannie lifted her head, whispering, "Reeny, what's the matter?"

Reeny slowly sat down on her bed, slipping off her high heels, letting them drop onto the rug by her bed as she answered, "Frannie, Tom's enlisted in the Army. He says he can't stay at school when so many other men are off fighting for his freedom. He says he can't stay home any longer and let others do a job he should be doing too. He will be leaving in two weeks. Frannie, my heart is breaking. What will I do without him? Please, Frannie, help me to be strong." Frannie was stunned. Here was her big sister, so sad, so confused. For the first time in Frannie's life, Reeny was coming to her for support. Reeny was always the one who guided Frannie. Reeny was the anchor, always assuring Frannie that all was right in the universe. It scared Frannie. She could see Reeny 's heart was aching. Frannie loved her sister and would do anything to help ease her pain. Frannie jumped off her bed, ran over to her sister and gathered Reeny into her arms. Reeny laid her head on Frannie's young shoulders and together they cried. Their idyllic world was changing. They were changing. Frannie wasn't sure how, but she felt things were different now. She was growing up. These two sisters were growing closer, reaching out to each other in these uncertain times.

CHAPTER 2

The women of this country rallied together, pulling on an untapped source of strength many did not know they possessed. A trickle down effect took place. Women became the family breadwinners. Older girls in the family became surrogate mothers providing the maternal love and care their younger siblings needed. Young boys at home took up the chores left undone by older brothers or fathers no longer at home. American families realized a war must be won, children must be fed, and life must go on.

Frannie's family was in with it along with everyone else. Mom and Dad, right along side other older couples, huffed and puffed while they shoveled the snow from their own walkways. Mom put on her glasses, her good hat and coat, and learned to drive the family Buick. Women could not afford to be dependent on men, for who knew when one would be called away. Women drove cars, balanced checkbooks, and worked in factories. Reeny got Mom a job in the law office where she worked. Clerking jobs, previously held by men, were now available to women who had learned to type and take shorthand. They were thankful these skills were subconsciously retained and easily resurfaced with practice. Much like riding a bicycle, a little practice and the skills were back up to speed in no time. Each morning Mom and Reeny, giggling like schoolgirls, piled into the Buick and drove off to the office. Dad grumped a little about being left behind to do what he called women's work, but secretly he liked the role reversal. He liked the freedom of having his days to himself, working at the pace he chose. There was a twinkle in his eye the day he managed to do the laundry and the white clothes came out pristine. He was a bit comical, eyeballing the hanging shirts, smiling with satisfaction at a job well done.

Reeny McFadden turned twenty-one years old that summer of 1944. She and her family saw some big changes that year. Tom had finished his basic training. Like tens of thousands of other enlisted men with frantic sweethearts soon to be left behind, he came home on leave before shipping out to foreign soil. Frannie watched from her upstairs dormer window as Tom and Reeny walked along the sidewalks, arms around each other's waist, heads bent close as they talked and laughed together. When Reeny wasn't at work, she and Tom were always together until late into the night, when Reeny would come quietly up the stairs so as not to wake anyone in the family. Many mornings Frannie would get up to find Tom asleep on the divan, having stayed so late, it was easier to spend the night. Tom took up all of Reeny's time and Frannie felt completely alone, abandoned by the sister she loved so much. So caught up in her love for Tom and the desperate sadness creeping into her life with Tom's imminent departure, Reeny seemed to forget Frannie existed. This hurt Frannie very much. Frannie tried to rationalize the loss of her sister's closeness, telling herself that Reeny was the one who needed comforting. Reeny was on the verge of being separated, perhaps forever, from the greatest love of her life. Frannie tried to be mature and accepting of the situation, but she failed. Perhaps it was because she was only fifteen years old and still in that selfish age group. She began to resent Tom's total absorption into her family. To Dad and Mom, Tom was the son they never had, and they doted on him. During these sunny days of summer, their lives centered around Tom and Reeny's involvement with each other.

Tom's father had died when Tom was still a baby. His mother raised Tom and his sister, May, by herself. She operated a boardinghouse upstate. Tom's mother died just after he graduated from high school. Tom's sister, May, was eight years older than Tom. May was widowed with two daughters of her own when their mother died. Since Tom had no family, except for his sister and nieces upstate, he spent his leave time with Reeny and her family. Even with his impending departure, those days with Tom around so much were memorable. Dad and Tom had male comraderie. Mom had a son to dote on. Reeny had the love of her life with her, and Frannie had a big brother. Everyone pushed Tom's inevitable leaving to the back of their minds, enjoying his presence, soaking up the joy and comfort he brought to a middle-aged couple, a love struck young woman, and an adoring teenage girl.

It was the weekend before Tom was due to ship out on Monday. Summer rain had been falling all day Saturday, keeping Frannie in the kitchen with Mom. Reeny and Tom had taken the Buick and gone upstate so Tom could say goodbye to his sister and nieces. Reeny was taking Tom directly to Ft. Benning after their visit with May. Mom worried about Reeny driving home all alone in the rain, after dropping Tom off at the base. But Reeny had insisted. She wanted this time alone with Tom and his small family, then a few precious hours to be alone together. Mom and Frannie were baking apple pies, late that Saturday afternoon. The kitchen smelled glorious with the cinnamon and apple fragrance. Rain was falling outside and evening slipped into darkness when into this quiet world came the shrill of the telephone ringing. "Mom, Mom, can you hear me, it's Reeny. Tom and I got married today. Oh, Mom, I'm so happy. I just wanted to call and tell you the wonderful news, and now we are going on upstate to see May and the girls. Mom, you are happy for me, aren't you? Oh, Mom, I am so happy. I can't put it into words. I'll see you when I get home on Monday. Tell Frannie and Dad my wonderful news. Oh, Mom, everything is wonderful. I'll see you later and I love you," said Reeny, as she hung up the telephone on her end of the long-distance line.

Mom moved in a stunned silence. "She and Tom got married" was all she could say to Frannie on her way to the living room, looking for Dad. Frannie slid off her stool and followed her mother. Dad was just clicking off the radio, realizing from the look on Mom's face, silence was needed as Mom said to him, "Well, they've gone and done it. That was Reeny. She and Tom got married today. Oh, Stan, I wish the world wasn't such a mess right now. I'm so afraid our girl's going to get hurt. And Tom, poor Tom. I just pray God protects him."

They both sat down on the divan, Dad taking Mom into his arms and saying, "Now, Stella, they're young and in love. There's a war on, they're going to be separated soon. They want to be married, to have something tangible to hang onto in this time of craziness. Tom's a good man. Our girl's got herself a good husband. I'm happy for them both. I just hope and pray God keeps our Tom safe and brings him home to our little girl. Now, dry up your tears, and let's go have some of that apple pie you and Frannie just baked. It's smells delicious. Do you have some ice-cream to put on top of it?" With his words, Dad put his seal of approval on things. The three of them went into the kitchen and ate their pie and ice-cream. They were quiet with their own thoughts of Tom and Reeny's new life together, yet for now, apart.

CHAPTER 3

With America's deep involvement in the war that year, everyone's minds and hearts were with their beloved "boys" overseas. Almost every family had a brother, son, husband, or father, involved someway with the war in Europe. Woman at home pitched in wholeheartedly, volunteering their time after long hours in offices or factories. No one had a home life anymore. Women went from work to volunteer centers. No one's hands went idle. Tons of cookies were baked, miles of bandages were rolled, and reams of letters were written, and all were packed lovingly into boxes and shipped overseas. Each woman's loneliness and fear for the safety of her beloved man was kept in check by the enormous amount of work being done on the home front. There was a sense of patriotic urgency, combined with a loving and sometimes humorous bond between these hardworking women left at home to run the county and provide loving support for their fighting menfolk stationed in faraway places of war. Frannie and Reeny would sit at the local Red Cross station rolling bandages for hours. As the women became familiar with each other, friendships were formed. The common denominators of work and grief soon leveled any social barriers that previously existed between the women. Women from all social backgrounds leaned on each other. The young women helped the older women do the hard physical labor they were not used to. In return, these older women shared their secrets of experience with their daughters and friends. Conversations about men, life, sex, childbirth, all previously taboo subjects, became acceptable discussion topics at working roundtables across America.

Early in the fall, a few weeks after Tom's departure, Reeny was putting Frannie's hair up in bobby pins, while sleet fell outside in the darkness. Their eyes met in the mirror and Reeny smiled softly and said, "Frannie, I have some wonderful news. I'm going to have a baby." Frannie turned around slowly, her heart swelling with happiness for her sister and said, "Reeny, I'm so happy for you. Just think, I'll be an auntie. Have you told Mom and Dad yet?"

"No, I thought I'd wait until I saw the doctor. Dr. Graham confirmed it today, so now I'll go down and tell the folks. Want to come with me?" Reeny said as she smiled slyly at Frannie. "Let's tease them a bit and make them guess the good news, shall we?" With arms around each other's waist and bobby pinned curls in their hair, both girls descended the stairs laughing and giggling, full of shared secrets and happiness.

Dad was sitting in his easy chair, his face hidden by the day's newspaper. Mom sat contentedly in her rocker, peacefully crocheting balls of red wool into warm neck scarves. Soft orchestra music hummed from the radio box. Into this cozy setting came the two sisters, both looking like cats that swallowed the canary. Mom looked up first, sensing an aura of excitement surrounding her two daughters. It took a couple of minutes before Dad realized his wife was staring up at his daughters. Not sure what was up but knowing something unusual was soon to take place, he gave his newspaper a quick shake, folded it in half, and laid it on the coffee table. He took off his glasses and sat up straighter in his easy chair. At the same time Mom stuck her crochet needle into her yarn and quietly laid the bundle on her lap. Frannie sat down on the divan, followed quickly by Reeny. It was as if Reeny needed the physical support of her younger sister, needed to be right next to her as she delivered her joyous, yet intimidating news to her parents. "Mom, Dad, I'm going to have a baby" blurted out Reeny, seemingly just as stunned as her parents by this revelation. Mom's eyebrows raised up an inch, causing her glasses to slide down her nose. Dad's head cocked backyards and suddenly he started laughing.

Jumping up, he grabbed Reeny into his arms, swinging her around like she was a little girl again as he said, "Oh my baby, my little girl, going to be a mother herself now. I am so happy for us all. Damn, I wish Tom were here! Does he know yet, Reeny?"

Sheepishly, Reeny looked up at her dad and said, "No, no, Dad, he doesn't know yet. I just found out for sure myself. Today the doctor confirmed it. I wanted to tell you and Mom just as soon as I was sure. I'll get a letter off to Tom right away, but it'll be weeks before he gets my letter."

In the midst of Dad and Reeny's excitement it became apparent that Mom was sitting very still and quiet. Reeny looked over at her mother and suddenly became quiet herself. She walked slowly over to Mom's rocker and sat down at her feet, laying her head on Mom's lap, pushing the red yard over. Mom began to slowly brush her fingers through Reeny's silky hair, softly running her fingertips across Reeny's forehead. Mom's hands were warm and comforting.

Concerned glances passed between Stan and Stella. Here was their baby, expecting a baby of her own in such uncertain, troubled times. But youth, being the eternal buffer against pain and experience, was hopeful and optimistic. Neither parent was going to show the slightest worry or doubt concerning their daughter's wonderful news. The McFadden family huddled together in the closeness of their home. Thoughts of this new life coming into their world created a myriad of images in each person's mind. Stan's heart was heavy, a mixture of joy and worry. This family of his, these three women and now this unborn life were all weighing heavy on his mind. These were worrisome times for Stan. There was no guarantee of Tom's safe return. There were so many fears being kept silent. In the midst of his trusting family, no voice was given to his worries. Putting a smile on his face and love in his eyes, he put his arms around his daughter who carried her unborn child. He walked her upstairs saying, "You have given me great joy, a new beginning, a new baby in the house after all these years. I'm sure Tom will be thrilled when he gets your news. Until Tom returns, your mom and I will be here for you and the baby. With God's help, Tom will be home soon. Reeny, be strong, there are no timelines during war. We will pray and we will be strong, and in the meantime we will get ready for your baby's arrival. Always remember how much I love you." With a kiss and a hug, Stan left her at her bedroom door and went on down the hall to his room to be alone with his thoughts.

CHAPTER 4

With so much commotion resulting from the war and the hurried marriage of Tom and Reeny, it was only natural that Frannie felt left out and pushed aside. With Reeny spending so much time, first with Tom, and then working with Mom at her office job, Frannie was left alone much of the time. Coming home from school to a cold, dimly lit house, with no one home yet, was depressing to Frannie. Before the war started, coming home from school was so wonderfully routine, coming into a warm house, lights on, radio playing softly, Mom starting dinner and the house smelling so good from her cooking. Now, coming home from school began to get more depressing as fall darkened the days. So instead of coming home, Frannie would walk home with her best friend, Janet Slocum. The Slocum household seemed unaffected by the war. Other than having the news on the radio each afternoon when Frannie and Janet walked in, their house seemed noisy with children, and Mrs. Slocum was usually in the kitchen cooking food that smelled of spices. Janet had a brother, two years older than she and Frannie, and the rest of Janet's siblings consisted of three younger sisters. With so many younger children at home, Mrs. Slocum was always busy, with her face flushed, and wispy curls of chestnut brown hair surrounding her face. She made the time to welcome Frannie and made her feel like she was part of the Slocum family. Mrs. Slocum even had a rollaway bed down in the basement she would pull out and put into Janet's bedroom for Frannie to sleep on whenever she spent the night. Frannie loved being part of this big, noisy family and began to stay at the Slocums' home often.

Frannie missed her intimate times with Reeny. Every since Reeny met Tom, she seemed so much more grown up. The six-year age difference between the girls seemed like a wider gap as Frannie was entering womanhood and Reenie had already been there for several years. Even with Tom's leaving, the closeness the girls had shared in the past did not return to them. Reeny seemed womanly, grown up, more like Mom. Reeny and Mom shared secrets that Frannie wasn't a part of. Since both Reeny and Mom were "married ladies," they seemed to have a lot of things to talk about and sometimes even blush and giggle about. During some of these times both women would glance sheepishly in Frannie's direction. Their conversation would halt. Sometimes they even left the room, acting like they were going into the kitchen to do something, and would continue their talks where Frannie could not hear the details. Frannie could understand they had married woman stuff, even sex, to talk about with each other. But she felt angry sometimes. They acted like she was still a little girl. It embarrassed her the way they would coyly slip out of the room when they wanted to discuss things they thought she didn't know anything about, like sex and babies. And it was true, she didn't. But their exclusion of her made her feel immature and unwanted, like she wasn't part of the family. She had no one to turn to. Dad would try to pacify her with platitudes such as "this too shall pass," but it wasn't passing. Reeny and Mom were getting closer with Tom being gone and Reeny going to have a baby. It seemed to Frannie that Mom and Reeny were wrapped up in a world that included just the two of them. They worked together, they rode together, they talked endlessly of husbands and babies. It was a world that Frannie could not enter, excluded by her youth and inexperience. So she leaned towards her friend and her friend's family. There was so much activity going on in the Slocum family that quiet little Frannie barely made an impact on the household. Mrs. Slocum actually welcomed her visits. Frannie was always polite and helpful with the younger girls. Even Tim, the only boy in the family, seemed to welcome Frannie's attention. With Frannie being fifteen years old and Tim already seventeen years old, the two could talk about the latest Big Band craze and what the kids at the local high school were up to. Tim was a senior and Frannie a sophomore with Janet, so it was quite an ego booster for Tim to seek out Frannie at school, walking her and Janet to their classes. Janet would make jokes about her brother never being seen with her until Frannie became her friend. But the three of them had fun, walking to classes, the two girls sharing laughs while watching Tim and the other senior boys practice football after school. Being friends with Janet meant she was included in the family's weekly trek to whatever high school campus the weekly football game was being played at. If it was a home game, Frannie and Janet would walk to the high school football field, meeting their other girlfriends, and end up with sore throats from screaming for their home team. When Tim traveled to other nearby high schools to play visitor games with his team, Frannie was overjoyed to pile into the Slocums' reliable 1939 Mercury, snuggling between Janet and her little sisters, happy and laughing, with frost on the windows and body warmth keeping five giggling girls in the backseat nice and warm.

Tim was star of his high school football team. He was a natural athlete, tall and slim, with a handsome face to top off a superb physique. He was also intelligent and studious. To make him even more perfect, he had charm and a wonderful sense of humor. Everyone liked Tim. He was a friend to all his classmates. He was liked and respected by their parents. His excellent grades earned him the praise of his teachers. His athletic accomplishments and the glory he brought to his school earned him the respect and honor of being a favorite of his coaches. Tim was even loved by his four little sisters. He was the perfect son, the perfect big brother, and the perfect student. In Frannie's young mind and heart, Tim was her idea of the perfect boyfriend. But Tim was consumed with his sports and his studies. He was working hard in high school. He was hoping to win a full-ride scholarship to Northwestern University. He had noticed what a cute little friend his sister Janet began bringing home, and as their friendship grew, he noticed Frannie was quickly becoming a regular addition to his already female dominated family. Tim considered his younger sister Janet a kid and Frannie fell into 'the kid' category also. Tim was surrounded with little sisters. One more girl was no big deal to him. He loved his family and adored his sweet sisters, so it was natural for him to like Frannie. He was used to being around females. He and his dad would often sneak down into the basement workshop. His dad called it their time to 'get away from the gaggle of females upstairs,' referring to his mom and his sisters. They would fix Mom's broken iron or wash machine while they listened to the war news on the crackling radio. Reception wasn't perfect in the basement, but it was good enough for the two men. It was the sharing of this time together that Tim and his dad enjoyed. They loved their womenfolk, but they needed their time alone together, and the basement workroom was off limits to the ladies of the house. It was during one of these times with his dad that Tim mentioned Janet's new friend being so much a part of the Slocum family. Glancing at Tim, his dad said, "Oh, you mean Frannie. Yea, she is a quiet thing compared to your sisters. I guess that's how you turn out if you come from a small family. As you know, Tim, a small family is pretty unusual. Your mom and I love each one of you kids, but it is hard to support a big family. But that's just the way it is with some couples. You know, Tim, you're getting pretty grown up yourself. The years have gone by so fast. I guess it's time I talked to you about, you know, family matters." Tim looked up at his father and almost laughed aloud. Mel Slocum was beat red, sweating, and his Adam's apple was bobbing up and down nervously. There really wasn't much about girls that Tim and the other boys at school hadn't already discussed. Tim had a girlfriend last year, one he had kissed and fondled on numerous occasions. Other than being in an uncomfortable position several times, they hadn't done much more than explore each other's bodies. He really didn't want to share this information with his dad, nor did he want his dad to share any information about his mom. That was not something a son wanted to hear about his mother. Tim refused to even imagine his parents as sexual human beings.

So, to avoid any embarrassing discussion on the subject of sex and to make sure he didn't learn anything more than he already knew about his mom and dad, he smiled sheepishly up at his dad and said, "That's okay, Dad. Me and the coach had this talk already. You know Coach Hubbell, he isn't gong to let his players get in any 'girl trouble' or get sick with any of those sex diseases."

Mr. Slocum stopped swallowing and said, "That's great, okay, okay, but if there is anything you need to know, you just let me know, son. You may think your dad is over the hill, but as you can see, me and your mom are pretty happy together." Even though this was a little more information than Tim wanted to hear, he had to admit his parents were very happy together and he was glad he was their son. So with Mel reassured that Tim's education in that area was taken care of, he breathed easier and went on with his busy life as husband and father of five children.

Soon after this time with his dad, Tim was hanging out in the town square with his football buddies when Janet and Frannie walked through the square, heading to the bookshop. The first snowfall wasn't completely shoveled off the walkway around the gazebo, so both girls were forced to lift up their skirts to step over piles of snow. The boys were treated to a revealing glimpse of the girls' upper thighs. Wolf howls erupted from the noisy boys, making the girls feel giddy and appreciated. The girls knew their reputations were at stake, so they quickly lowered their skirts, acting insulted and mortified by the boys' howls. While Tim enjoyed looking at Frannie's well-shaped thigh, he was mortified the other boys were oogling his sister. He jokingly slugged his pals, saying in a rough voice, "Hey, guys, that's my little sister and her friend. They're just kids. Heck, they're not even developed yet."

This brought out a burst of laughter from some of the guys, with his best friend Pete speaking up, "Where have you been, Tim? Your sister's a real knockout. She's beautiful, and her friend Frannie, well, are you blind or what? She's sexy."

Tim felt the need to stick up for his sister and her friend. With an angry look on his face, he rounded on Pete saying, "You just quit looking at my sister. She's just a kid and so is her friend." Tim ran over to where the two girls were just entering the bookstore. After closing the door against the cold, the three of them took off their mittens, walked up to the wood stove and put their hands over the warm stove. Tim looked at Frannie and Janet and said, "Sorry, girls, my buddies didn't mean to be rude. They're just immature. But I set them straight. They know now not to whistle at my sister, or at you either, Frannie." Frannie started to giggle and Tim looked over at her. He sucked his breath in when he saw her flushed face. His friends were right. Where had he been, or where had his eyes been? She was sexy. Her cheeks were flushed from the cold, her eyes were wet and sparkling, snow melting on her long lashes. Then he noticed her lips. They were full and pink and soft looking. All of this beauty in such a young, innocent, pixie-looking face. It took him a moment to remember he was looking at Frannie.

Frannie looked up at Tim as he was talking. Suddenly there was this strange feeling in her heart, a kind of fluttery feeling. She hadn't really noticed Tim as a guy. She had only seen him as Janet's brother. He was always nice to her, but he was nice to everyone, especially his little sisters. Up until this moment she had always felt like one of his sisters. But this feeling in her heart was not a feeling you had for someone in your family. She dearly loved her mom, her dad, Tom, and Reeny, but she had never felt this flutter in her heart when she thought of them. It was new, and it felt strange but nice. For the first time, she actually looked straight into Tim's eyes and saw him as a person. He was handsome, alive and vibrant, caring about her and Janet. Her heart swelled and she felt glad that he cared enough about her to protect her reputation when his friends were oogling her and whistling at her.

She smiled sweetly at Tim and said, "Thank you, Tim. I don't think they meant any harm, but it's nice to know we have you to protect us if we need it. Besides Tom and my dad, I never had a boy stick up for me before. I like it."

Janet, standing next to Frannie, warming her hands over the wood stove, watched Tim and her friend and could tell something unusual was happening. It was a little worrisome. She always had all of Frannie's attention. Mom teased them, saying they were like two peas in a pod. She felt like Tim was coming into a circle that before today, only she and Frannie inhabited. But she loved Tim and she loved her best friend Frannie, so she kept quiet, thinking perhaps she was seeing too much in their conversation. Her mom always said she made a mountain out of a molehill and maybe that's what she was doing with Tim and Frannie. So she smiled at Tim and thanked him for being such a good big brother.

The three of them stood by the wood stove warming up. They read the latest newspaper headlines, bemoaning the casualties of the war. Both Janet and Tim were careful about discussing the war around Frannie. They knew she had a brother-in-law fighting in Europe. They also knew Frannie's older sister, the one married to the soldier, was going to have a baby next summer. It was a long way off, and with the eternal optimism of youth, they all hoped the war would end soon and bring Frannie's sister's husband home to his family.

Frannie spent much of her time at the Slocum house. Her family did not seem to have much time to give to Frannie since Tom went away. Even now Frannie had made arrangements to spend the weekend with the Slocums. Mom, Dad, and Reeny had plans to travel upstate to get to know Tom's sister better. May, Tom's sister, and her two daughters were Tom's only living family and Reeny wanted them all to be close, so the new baby would know his or her auntie and cousins. They were leaving tonight, driving up north, and coming back Sunday so Mom and Reeny would be back for work on Monday. Sometimes Frannie thought her family was relieved to have her spend so much time with the Slocums. Mom and Dad seemed so involved with Reeny and making sure she was happy and healthy and didn't worry over Tom being away. It took up all Mom and Dad's time making sure Reeny was as happy as she could be, considering her husband was away fighting in the war.

Mom and Dad had met Janet and her family and liked them. They were glad Frannie had a friend with such a nice family and was willing to share her family with Frannie. They were comforted knowing Frannie had Janet and her sisters to keep her company. They liked Janet's older brother, thinking him a fine young man, so protective of his sisters and of Frannie too. It seemed a perfect solution at a time when their older daughter required so much of their time and attention. Frannie was still so young. They were completely involved with their older, married daughter, who was now expecting her first baby. They were doing their best to keep Reeny comforted, making sure she didn't get depressed over Tom's absence, making sure she didn't worry about Tom, making sure she stayed healthy for her sake and her baby's sake. It seemed there was so much about Reeny's life to worry about right now, they just didn't want to have to include Frannie in these grown up issues. They rationalized that Frannie was still young and should be enjoying a carefree high school life. It was easier to let her blend in with the Slocum's large and loving family. They reassured themselves by knowing how much help Frannie was to Mrs. Slocum. Their Frannie was sweet natured, helpful, polite, and loved the little Slocum girls. It seemed like an ideal situation for both families at this time.

The setting sun was beginning to spread a pink glow over the snow as Frannie, Janet, and Tim left the bookstore and headed back to the Slocum's house. As the three of them left the bookstore, Frannie looked at the sky and its pink glowing clouds. These were what Reeny called 'God Clouds.' They formed when the sun was setting enough to make the clouds look pink and puffy and rolling all over the sky. Reeny said it looked like pictures of the clouds in the Bible so she called them 'God Clouds.' Just at this moment, Frannie felt very lonely; she missed her family. She didn't quite know how she had become so separated from them. It seemed like Reeny and Mom and Dad were a family, and she was on the outside looking in at the three of them. The three of them seemed like a group, so concerned with Reeny, the new baby, and Tom away in Europe. She didn't fit in anymore. She was still a kid, still in high school. She wasn't supposed to be worried about war, or wives left behind, or babies. She was supposed to be having fun, giggling over boys, agonizing over test scores, learning the latest dances, listening to Big Bands, not war news. She felt like she belonged with the Slocums. They were always noisy, laughing together and picking out skirts and sweaters to mix and match and share. The war hadn't taken anyone from the Slocum's family. She shivered in the cold. Tim noticed and put his arm around her shoulder and around Janet's shoulder, saying

.ter keep his sister and her friend warm or he'd catch heck from
⌐ . Frannie had a strange desire to lay her head on Tim's shoulder
but instinct made her realize she shouldn't do that while Janet was
with them. Before today, Frannie had never really thought of Tim as
'a guy,' but she liked this feeling of being close to him, having him
stick up for her when the other boys whistled at her. It made her feel
important to Tim. It also made her realize that she was a girl and
intuitively she knew Tim looked at her as a girl, not as a sister. It was
a heady feeling, this feminine giddiness, combined with power over
a man's feelings. She wondered if this was how Reeny felt with Tom.
She felt happy and content walking along the slushy road back to the
Slocums. She would be there all weekend and now she realized she
would have all weekend with Tim. She never thought of it like that
before. Tim was just there, part of the Slocum family. Suddenly
Frannie realized she was very glad that Tim was part of the Slocum
family.

"Get in here, you three. It's getting dark. Go stand by the fire and
get warm, and take those snow boots off in the wanigan. I don't want
snow tracked into the house. Supper is almost ready. Mel, come up
here and wash up for dinner. Girls, girls, put those dolls away and get
cleaned up for dinner." Marge Slocum's flushed face and unruly hair
met the three teenagers at the front porch door, serving spoon waving
in the air as Marge issued orders to her entire family.

The walk through town had made Frannie, Tim, and Janet
ravenous. They tossed boots, mittens, coats and scarves on the bench
in the wanigan and headed to the dining room table. Scoops of
mashed potatoes and gravy combined with crispy fried chicken
disappeared from everyone's plates. "Darn good dinner, Marge,"
said Mel Slocum. This praise was echoed around the table.

"Thank you, Honey," replied Marge in absentminded way. "It's
time we turned on the Audiovox. I want to hear the latest news. It's
not going too good for our troops in Europe. Oh my, I'm sorry,
Frannie. Me and my big mouth. I'm sure your Tom is fine. I wished
this damn war was done with."

Poor Mrs. Slocum flushed a deep red at her unusual swearing. All
the family was quiet. Mom must be upset if she swore. Things must

be bad to get a cuss word out of Mom's mouth. Mr. Slocum glanced around the table at his surprised children and took over as he said, "Okay, Ma Slocum, you set yourself over there in your rocker next to the Audiovox. You little ones lie down on the rug by the fire. Me, Tim, Frannie and Janet will do up the dinner dishes while we listen to the news. Okay now, let's get going." Chairs scraped backwards, little girls grabbed pillows and afghans off the divan and headed for the braided rug in front of the fire. Mrs. Slocum smiled up at her husband and walked over to her rocking chair, switching on the radio as she sat down. She turned it up loud enough so you could hear it over the clatter of dishes being washed. Soft dance music rolled out over the big room that contained kitchen, dining area, and living room. Mrs. Slocum leaned her head back and closed her eyes, enjoying the music. The little girls snuggled together on the rug, snapping their fingers to the beat of the music. Mel, Tim, Janet, and Frannie worked on washing and drying the dishes. Suddenly Mel swooped Janet into his arms and began dancing with her across the kitchen linoleum. With a dishtowel slung over his shoulder, Tim reached over and put his hand on Frannie's waist and his other hand on her shoulder, and off they went gliding around the kitchen in time with the music. The little girls sat up and started laughing at their dad and brother and sister acting silly and dancing in the kitchen. Taken by surprise, Frannie quickly recovered and started dancing with Tim. The whole family seemed to be in a festive mood. The ballroom tune was quickly followed by fast instrumental swing dance tune. Tim laughed and began jitterbugging with Frannie, who was a great little dancer herself. Laughing and twirling and clapping, they danced around the kitchen until the song ended. Both Tim and Frannie dropped into the chairs by the dinette table, exhausted but happy. The whole family was clapping.

"My gosh, Frannie and Tim, you two can cut a rug. Where'd you learn to jitterbug like that?" asked Mrs. Slocum.

"Reeny taught me," answered Frannie breathlessly.

"I practiced down in the basement," admitted a very cocky Tim, as he smiled admiringly at Frannie and said, "We'll have to practice more often. Frannie, you are a great dancer."

Shyly lowering her eyes, Frannie responded, "Thank you, Tim, I'd like that."

Later that night as Frannie lie in bed next to Janet, she had this tingly feeling in her stomach when she thought of the way Tim had held her in his arms when they danced. She remembered feeling his hips and his leg against her body as he held her close while they danced earlier in the kitchen. She got a warm sensation in her lower stomach when she thought about Tim's body. In her youth and innocence she had the dreamy sensation of living in a fairy tail. She loved being a part of this wonderful family that included a handsome prince charming who danced like Fred Astaire and made her feel like Cinderella. It had been a perfect evening, finishing the dishes together and then dancing with Tim while Janet danced with her father. She loved the way she felt when Tim held her in his strong arms. She loved being part of the Slocum family.

Later, the news had come on the radio. The mood in the Slocum household changed from silly happiness to concentrated silence. The war was escalating. Casualties were high. It was a part of life Frannie did not want to have to think about when she was with the Slocum family. She heard enough about the war when she was in her own home. Daily, she dealt with Reeny's fear over Tom's safety. She didn't want the war and the sorrow it caused to intrude on her life here at the Slocums. This was her make-believe life, her escape from the uncertainty and the barely submerged fear that was part of every day around Reeny. She was tired of being sad and worried and afraid. She wanted her sister to be happy but knew she wouldn't be until Tom returned home safe. Frannie wanted that to be a different part of her life. She wanted to go away from it once in a while. She wanted to come to the Slocums' where she could pretend she was part of their family. She could be happy in their home, where the war had not intruded so brutally. She had this wonderful new thrill when she was around Tim. It was as if her world was perfect as long as she was here in the Slocums' house. She fell asleep thinking of how Tim's arms felt around her while they were dancing. She was content and happy. She fell into a deep, satisfying sleep.

CHAPTER 5

The next day she woke up feeling rested yet excited. She felt like there was so much to look forward to, and the feeling made her giddy with unknown expectations. She dressed, brushed her hair, put on a little makeup and realized she was looking forward to going downstairs and seeing Tim. She hoped Janet didn't notice any change in her. She knew she better not act boy crazy around Tim. The Slocums considered her to be like a sister to Tim. She knew they wouldn't want any girl-likes-boy silliness going on in their home. The house seemed unusually quiet as she made her way downstairs. Janet wasn't in bed when Frannie woke up, but she figured Janet was already downstairs helping her mom with the little girls. She went into the kitchen. The early morning sun was flooding into the room, spreading an array of rainbow prisms across the kitchen linoleum as it struck the icicles hanging off the roof eve and reflected onto the white floor. The colorful beauty made Frannie gasp with delight. Suddenly Frannie heard a laugh from behind her as she whirled around and saw Tim getting a cup of coffee from the pot simmering on the stovetop. "Beautiful icicle rainbow, isn't it, sunshine?" asked Tim, as he brought his coffee over to the dinette table.

"Yes, it is," replied Frannie, as she helped herself to a cup of coffee. Usually she had hot cocoa, but she was feeling very grown up at the moment, so she decided to brave her first cup of coffee. She sat down by Tim and watched him add milk and sugar to his coffee, so she did the same. She took a swallow and almost spit it out but managed to get it down safely. She glanced at Tim, who hadn't noticed her grimace, and quickly pasted a smile on her face.

"Where is everyone? I've never been here when your house was so quiet," said Frannie.

"Well, sleepyhead," replied Tim, "Mom and Dad took the girls into the city to get them each a new fall dress. This first snowfall

Mom realize summer is gone and she better get the girls some warmer dresses. And since I didn't need or want a new dress and you were sound asleep like Rip Van Winkle, they went off without us. But I promised them I would keep you company today, so what do you want to do today?"

It took a moment for Frannie to realize she and Tim were alone together in the Slocums' house and he was going to entertain her for the entire day. This realization was exciting and scary at the same time. She had Tim all to herself. With her new feelings for Tim, this made her very happy. Frannie was sure Tim had no idea of her new awareness of him as a man, not a brother. She thought she should keep this discovery to herself for the time being.

The two of them finished breakfast and decided to go sledding. There was new snow on the hill up the road from the Slocums' house. Tim got the sled out of the basement. He oiled the runner and retied the rope handle. Tim and Frannie bundled up in their snow boots, coats, and mittens. They left the house with Tim pulling the sled behind them. "Not a whole lot of snow just yet," remarked Tim as he and Frannie trudged up Old Hill Road. "But I think there's enough to get a decent ride down. Are you up to trying it with me?" asked Tim.

"Of course, I'm no sissy," replied Frannie.

At the top of Old Hill Road, Tim positioned the sled and held it in place as Frannie got on in the front. She pulled her knees up to her chest while Tim got on behind her, then they both put their legs out to the sides of the sled. Frannie held the rope handle and Tim put his arms around Frannie's waist, hugging her close, and said softly in her ear, "I'm taking my chances, letting a woman drive, but I'm feeling extremely adventurous today. Let's go!" Tim dug his feet into the snow and pushed the sled off down the hill. There was just barely a covering of new snow, but it was fresh and it was enough. The sled took off and gained speed going down. Frannie and Tim went flying down the hill. Tim held tightly onto Frannie's waist while Frannie, laughing and handling the rope, maneuvered the sled through the trees like an expert. "I'm impressed," laughed Tim, as they narrowly rounded a small boulder in their path. They headed toward the wide meadow at the bottom of the hill, faces flushed, lungs bursting with fresh air, laughing so hard tears were running down their faces. Suddenly the rope flew out of Frannie's hand and the sled made a hard right turn, dumping them both off into the snow. They were far enough down the hill so their speed was not too great, and they rolled into the snow laughing hysterically. As they ran out of breath, they came to rest face to face in the snow looking into each other's eyes.

The sky above was expansive and light powder blue. The snow was hard and cold and crackly, but Frannie and Tim were warm and bundled up in their woolen coats. They lay there staring at each other, not even aware of the cold. Time stood still. It was so quiet, not a bird in the blue sky, not a soul around in the snow covered meadow. It was as if they were the only two people in the world. Frannie held her breath as Tim lifted his head and bent over her face and put his lips on hers. His lips were warm and full and soft. She closed her eyes and she felt like she was floating. Tim kissed her lips harder and she felt his tongue touch her lips, so she opened her mouth a little. He tasted so good and she felt so warm and silky. This was her first kiss and it seemed to last for hours. Then all too soon, Tim pulled his mouth away from hers. He stayed lying in the snow looking at her. He just stared at her face, looking confused. Finally he spoke to her, "Frannie, I'm sorry if I scared you. I couldn't help it. I wanted to kiss you so much. You are so pretty and so sweet. You make me feel so strange inside. It feels so good to be near you." He took off his mitten and reached over and rubbed her face, her eyes, and her lips. Then he bent down again and kissed her deeply, pushing into her mouth with his tongue. He slipped his cold hand inside her coat trying to warm it, and at the same time feeling the shape and outline of her breast. His touching her breast caused a warm sensation to flow between her legs. She had never felt like this before and she didn't want it ever to end. Finally Tim pulled away again. "I think we better go home, Frannie. This feels so good, but I think we better stop now."

It took them a couple of hours to walk home pulling the sled behind them. Neither one seemed to be in a hurry. They walked slowly, holding hands, smiling at each other and stopping to kiss

31

again along the way. It was a new discovery for both of them, this happiness they felt being with each other. It was exhilarating, to be together, to be so happy with each other, and to be alone with these new feelings. There was no one to watch their discovery unfold, no one they had to hide their feelings from. They were able to kiss and hug and hold hands and not one other person was watching them. As they neared town and headed to the Slocums, they moved apart from each other, aware that their new feelings for each other would have to be a secret. They both knew it would be impossible for Frannie to remain within the family circle if Mr. or Mrs. Slocum discovered how they felt about each other. The family was still in the city when Frannie and Tim reached home. The house was quiet as they went up the front steps and into the wanigan. They sat on the bench and took off their coats, caps, mittens, and boots, leaving puddles of water on the mudroom floor. Frannie followed Tim down the hall as he headed toward the basement door.

"Let's go down to the basement and listen to my dad's radio down in his workshop. We can dance down there if some good band music comes on," Tim said invitingly.

Frannie followed him down the steep stairs into the dim basement. Tim clicked on the overhead light and the bulb flooded the cement block room with light. The basement smelled musty, but it was warm and cozy. There was plenty of floor space to dance on even if it was just a concrete slab with rugs thrown down on it. The Slocums' old, tattered divan occupied one wall of the basement and Mr. Slocum's workbench ran the length on the opposite wall. The radio was perched on a sturdy shelf above the workbench. Tim went over and turned on the radio and dance music filled the basement. He walked over to Frannie, made a silly bow, and said, "Mademoiselle, may I have this dance with you?"

Frannie, blushing and smiling, replied, "Of course, kind sir," and off they twirled. Tim held her close, one arm around her waist, her head resting on his shoulder. Down in the quiet basement, it seemed like there was no one else in the world and time stood still. They danced a couple of slow dances and then the announcer came on giving a patriotic war bonds pitch, so they sat down on the divan. Frannie didn't know if it was the radio announcer talking about the war bonds or just the quiet mood down in the secluded basement, but suddenly she felt sad and a little afraid. She wanted Tim to hold her and kiss her and make the outside world go away. Tim was getting a little melancholy himself with his newfound desire for Frannie. He liked this feeling of being needed by someone so adoring and sweet. They moved closer together on the divan and looked into each other's eyes. Suddenly they were kissing and holding each other.

Perhaps it was the quiet of the basement or knowing they were the only two people in the house, but their aroused passion for the each other was too new for either of them to comprehend or control. Tim knew he should stop himself, but Frannie was in his arms, her body young and soft and inviting. Tim was a virgin himself, but his body knew what he wanted and instinct took over. He kissed Frannie, and stroking her breasts, slowly and lovingly removed her clothing and his. Frannie was more than willing to have Tim love her, to be her first, to show her what it was like to be loved. Perhaps she wanted to be like her sister Reeny, to have a man who loved her in the same way Tom loved Reeny. In Frannie's young mind, she didn't stop to think how different their circumstances were. She only knew she was lonely and her body was feeling passions never before aroused. In her innocence, she had only a vague notion that what she was doing might have far reaching consequences. The only thing important to her in this basement with Tim holding her was to be as close to Tim as she could. She laid down on the scratchy divan, not even feeling the rough material beneath her buttocks. Tim had removed their clothing and he was poised just inches above her. He was kissing her, his tongue everywhere inside her mouth. The feeling between her legs was exquisite. She could feel moisture between her thighs. Suddenly she felt Tim's hard penis rub against her pubic hair. Instinctively, she spread her legs allowing the tip of Tim's penis to push between her lower lips. She spread her legs wider and arched her back, not knowing how she knew, but instinctively knowing she wanted his penis inside her between her legs. She wanted something hard to rub inside her to take away the ache that was building within her. Tim's penis entered her, stopped momentarily by her virginity, then shoved through her, painful for just a moment. She felt him move back and forth inside her for a few seconds. She clung to him. He was kissing her mouth and moaning. The pleasure she was feeling between her legs was something she never imagined. She experienced her first orgasm as only a young virgin could, quickly and without shame, enjoying only the pleasure without considering anything beyond the moment. Then it was over. Tim's breathing slowed down. Her mind floated back down from the basement ceiling and the throbbing sensation between her legs began to subside. Tim lifted his head and looked at her. "Oh, Frannie, that was wonderful. It was the best feeling I've ever had in my life. You are so beautiful. I hope I didn't hurt you. Did you like it too? I've never been with anyone and I know you haven't either. I think I must love you to feel this way. Frannie, I know this wasn't supposed to happen between you and me, but I couldn't help it. I feel something very special for you. I think I have since you came into my family. I just didn't know how strong it was until this weekend. I know you like me. I think you are the most beautiful and sweetest girl I've ever met and I want to be with you always. We weren't very careful. I know you don't know what I mean, but I'll take care of things next time. You do want to be with me again, don't you, Frannie?" pleaded Tim. He was talking so much and so fast. She couldn't comprehend everything he was saying. Frannie wasn't sure what Tim meant by taking care of things. Her mother had been so busy with Reeny, she hadn't taken the time to thoroughly explain the details about sex with Frannie. Of course Frannie knew a girl could get pregnant from having sex with a boy, but surely that must happen after having sex many times. Even Reeny had told her she and Tom had sex many times before he went away, so Frannie didn't think having a baby came from having sex just once. She looked into Tim's pleading eyes, gently reassuring him that she was his girl. They got up from the divan, both a little embarrassed by their nakedness but smiling and giggling with their newfound pleasure.

Tim was experiencing a nagging concern about not using any contraceptive, but in his innocence he, like Frannie, figured once was not going to result in a baby. He silently vowed to himself to get with the guys and find out where he could buy something that would keep Frannie from getting pregnant. They were both too young to have that worry. Besides, his parents and his coach had big plans for him and his scholarship. He was graduating midterm and expected to be at Northwestern by February. That was only four months away. He would talk to his friends right away. He wanted to be intimate with Frannie again before he went away. Northwestern was close enough that he could come home sometimes and visit her. Right now, still basking in the glow of his first sexual experience, Tim thought his life was great.

After they both dressed, they turned off the radio, straightened the afghan on the old divan, and headed upstairs. They were both famished. Frannie felt so grown up. She was alone in the house with Tim. She enjoyed acting like a married woman, first down in the basement with Tim, and now in the kitchen heating up leftover fried chicken for her and Tim. It would be hours before the Slocums came home. She and Tim had the rest of the day with the house all to themselves. After eating and cleaning up the kitchen, they went back outside and played in the snow, scraping up the sparse layer of snow on the ground into a makeshift snowman for the little girls to laugh at when they got home.

Long after the sun went down, the Mercury headlights appeared in the driveway and the house was filled with excited girls, all wanting to show their big brother the wonderful new winter dresses they had picked out. Soon Frannie was caught up in the girlish pleasure of new dresses. She and Janet went off to Janet's bedroom to see if Janet's new dress would fit Frannie since they were both about the same size. Once in the bedroom, Frannie was hesitant about undressing in front of Janet, afraid there would be some sign on her lost virginity. But Janet was far too tired to notice anything unusual about her friend. As expected, the dress fit both girls perfectly and Janet generously offered to lend her new dress to

Frannie anytime she wanted to borrow it. Both girls went to bed happy in their friendship. Frannie was perhaps the happier girl, having both her friendship with Janet and her newfound romance with Janet's brother, Tim. As she lay quietly beside Janet, she relived the moments of love she and Tim shared down in the basement. Frannie fell asleep happy and contented.

CHAPTER 6

Later that night, long after everyone else in the house was asleep, Mel Slocum heard his dogs barking excitedly at a car pulling up the driveway. Loud knocking brought Mr. And Mrs. Slocum, wearing their flannel wrappers and slippers, out into the wanigan to answer the porch door. It was freezing cold and pitch black outside. Mr. Slocum flipped on the outside bulb to reveal a disheveled man, shaking and pale. It took several minutes before they recognized Frannie's father, Stan. They were shocked at his appearance, but something in his eyes quieted them until they could help Stan into their home and get him warmed up. Taking Stan by the arm, Marge Slocum guided him down the long hallway and into the kitchen. She quietly put the coffee pot on the stove and lit the flame. Mel Slocum, sensing that something was terribly wrong, closed the door to the kitchen. The three adults sat at the Formica dinette, waiting for the coffee to percolate. Finally Stan rubbed his eyes, and the tears began to fall. He barely got out the words "Tom's been killed" before he broke down completely, sobbing into his folded arms on the cold tabletop.

Frannie woke up slowly, feeling Mrs. Slocum's hand shaking her. Janet's bedroom was still dark. "Wake up, Frannie, your dad's come to pick you up," whispered Mrs. Slocum, careful to keep her voice low so as not to wake Janet or her little sister.

"But, Mrs. Slocum, it's still night time," replied a half asleep Frannie, as she pulled herself from beneath the pile of warm blankets.

"I know, Frannie, but you need to go home. Come on and get dressed. I'll get your stuff together and meet you in the kitchen," whispered Mrs. Slocum, and she quietly left the bedroom. Frannie was awake enough now to realize it must be early Sunday morning. Her parents and Reeny weren't due home until late Sunday night. A sick feeling began to grow in the pit of her stomach as she dressed quickly and went into the Slocums' kitchen. She was shocked to see her father sitting at the table in the Slocums' kitchen. One glance at her dad and she knew her whole world was about to change. Her stalwart father, always the strong, kind, quiet man that everyone leaned on, sat at the Slocums' kitchen table, a completely broken man. She began to tremble as she sat down in the chair next to him. She looked into his warm brown eyes, so sad and tear filled. He shook his head and tried to gain control over his emotions as he looked at his younger daughter.

"Frannie, we need you to come home now. There's been some very bad news to deal with," said Dad, as he stood up and pulled Frannie into his arms. "Tom's not coming back to us, Frannie. He's given his life to protect us and fight for our freedom. Now it's our job to be as strong as we can be for your sister."

Frannie tried to absorb what Dad was saying, but there was a loud ringing in her ears and a tremendous ache in her chest where she thought her heart was. Mrs. Slocum helped her put on her woolen coat as Dad guided her out the front door. As she walked down icy porch steps to Dad's waiting Buick, she heard Mr. Slocum talking to Dad. "Now, Stan, you call us anytime. You let us know if there is anything, anything at all, we can do. You folks are like family to us now. We all have to stick together and hold each other up in these tragic times. My heart aches for your girl, Reeny. Frannie is welcome here anytime. She's like one of my own. Bye now."

Dad and Frannie drove along the icy, dark road, neither one talking, both lost in their own thoughts. Frannie, too young to have experienced any kind of sorrow, did not know if she could stand this ache in her heart and numb feeling in her head. For a moment she wondered if she might possibly die from this intense sorrow. Through the fog in her head she heard Dad telling her how they were having dinner at May's house last night when the doorbell rang and three army personnel had come into the house, followed by Tom's sister, May. These military personnel had quickly assessed the situation and realized they had all of Tom's immediate family, including his new bride, together in one place. In a way they must have considered it a blessing to only have to tell the heartbreaking news one time. They had sought out Dad as the head of the family and took him and May aside to deliver the tragic news. The highest ranking officer, an army major, had not shirked his duty to Tom's wife. He had gone personally up to Reeny, and taking her hands softly into his own, had delivered the words every military wife lives in fear of hearing. "I am grieved to have to tell you, Mrs. St. Clair, your husband was killed in action while serving in the armed forces of the United States of America." Dad said the officer had gone on to relate the details of Tom's death, but Reeny was beyond hearing or comprehending what the Major was telling her. Dad had taken his devastated daughter into his arms, trying somehow to cushion the blow, wishing over and over it had been him, not Tom, who was taken away from Reeny. May, suffering overwhelming shock and grief herself, managed to keep her sorrow within herself long enough to thank the army officers for delivering the news to Tom's family personally and showed them out the door.

The initial shock of this news and the ensuing grief was temporarily pushed away as Dad explained to Frannie that a funeral must be held with a final burial that would lay Tom's body to rest. Tom's soul was eternally with the Lord, but his body was en route home for a proper military funeral. May remained upstate with her young daughters, awaiting the return of Tom's body to his hometown. Dad, Mom, and Reeny had returned home to gather clothing and to pick up Frannie. They would spend Sunday packing to return upstate for Tom's funeral. May was taking care of the arrangements. Tom's body was due to arrive by train from New York City on Tuesday. May would handle the body's transfer from the railway station to the funeral parlor. The church service and burial were planned for Friday. When the law firm opened on Monday morning, Mom would call and explain the situation and let Mr. Sweeney, the senior partner, know that she and Reeny would not be in to work all week.

As they pulled up to their house, Frannie did not feel like the same girl who had left this same house just two days ago. So much had happened. She was not the same young, naïve adolescent who had packed her pajamas with so much anticipation at spending the weekend with her best girlfriend. As she walked up the front steps, she was a young woman with a heavy, sad heart. Somewhere back in her mind she vaguely wondered how someone could change, and so much happen in just the short space of two days. It seemed like months had passed, not just the beginning of a weekend. The weekend was not even finished yet. It did not seem real. She felt like she was watching through the window of someone else's house. With her numb mind and aching heart, she followed Dad into the house. It was dark and quiet. She went up to her room to find Reeny lying on her bed facing the wall. She was laying under the white eyelet quilt with her clothes still on. Her emerald green eyes stared vacantly at Frannie, as she chewed on her lower lip. Pausing just a moment, she whispered to Frannie, "He's gone, Frannie, my husband is gone. My heart is dead. It's with Tom. I don't even want to be in this world anymore, not without him."

"Oh, Reeny," cried Frannie, as she knelt beside the bed, laying her cheek next to Reeny's. Putting her arm over Reeny's shaking shoulders, she said through her own tears, "No, no, Reeny, you must hang on. You have the baby to think of."

Reeny turned her tear streaked face towards Frannie and said, "It's not enough, not without Tom. He didn't even know about his baby. I just shared the news with May the same day the officers came and told us about Tom. How could I have such joyous news to share with May, only to be followed later that same day by the most horrible news anyone could be told? What kind of God plays a cruel joke like that on people? I can't feel anything now, Frannie. I'm completely numb with this pain in my heart." Reeny buried her tear streaked face into her pillow.

Frannie stood up, unable to console her older sister. She could only stand by watching the torment her sister was suffering. She walked over to the other side of the bedroom and lay down on her bed, trying to make sense of the jumble of emotions whirling through her mind and heart. On the surface, as she lay there, she seemed calm and tired. Inside her head nothing made sense. She had become a woman, losing her virginity to Tim. She had suffered the news of the death of her beloved brother-in-law. He was the first person she had ever loved and then lost so suddenly. None of it made any sense or even seemed real for that matter. She did the only thing she could do. She laid down on her bed, blotted all the confusion and emotion out of her mind and fell asleep.

Several hours later, in the quiet afternoon, Mom awakened the two sisters. She gently shook them, telling them to get up, wash their faces and hands and come downstairs for some dinner. Although it seemed unimaginable under the circumstances, both girls were surprised they were actually hungry. They had slept all day without eating anything. Their hearts were numb, but their stomachs were still demanding sustenance. As this small family sat around the kitchen table, each lost in their own pain, they quietly made their plans for the coming week.

Mom called the law firm on Monday and she and Reeny were offered the genuine condolences of Mr. Sweeney and the other partners, along with time off for however long was needed to bury their fallen soldier. The family finished packing late Monday afternoon and headed out the driveway for the five-hour drive upstate to Tom's hometown. Reeny was lost in a world only she occupied. Her eyes glistened with unshed tears, yet when you looked into them there was no life there, just a glazed, uncomprehending look. She answered questions when asked but otherwise she was completely silent, locked in a pain-filled world. They arrived at May's late at night. The little girls were already in bed when May met them at the door and ushered them into her house. It was small, but very warm and cozy. She led them up a steep stairway to an attic that had been finished off to use as an additional room. There were two full size beds made up to accommodate them. All four travelers were quiet, sad, and weary. With a sweet smile and moist eyes, May welcomed Frannie into her heart, her home, and her family. In that warm, musty attic, five newly bound people grieved the loss of husband, brother, son-in-law and father-to-be. What a tremendous price this war was extracting from the vulnerable people left at home.

Tuesday morning arrived crisp and cold. It was the beginning of November, 1944. Tom's body was shipped home just as the war was winding down in Europe. His death was such a tragic sacrifice so near the end of the war. Reeny felt desolate, as if Tom's death was in vain. She momentarily wondered if his short stint in the Army had accomplished nothing except his loss. She tried hard not to let these futile, bitter feelings eat at her heart. But it was only this bitterness that had the ability to pierce the numbness in her heart. As these depressing feelings took hold of Reeny, it became harder for her to remember there was a new life growing beneath this heart that had become a rock.

With a heart numbed by pain and anguish, this young war widow accompanied her sister-in-law to the train station to accept the flag draped coffin wherein lay her beloved young husband. With her family beside her, she did her duty as so many other war widows had done before her. At Tom's funeral she stood proud and tall as she watched the patriotically decorated coffin holding her young husband's body descend into the dark abyss, taking him away from her and their unborn child. Never again would she find joyous rapture in his strong arms. She missed him with every fiber of her being. She would never know how she lived through that cold November day, accepting the flag, listening to the deafening gun salute, dropping the hothouse white orchid onto Tom's coffin as the first dark grains of earth were thrown onto her beloved, separating him for her forever. As lonely as any human being could be, Reeny tucked away her heart, lifted her pain filled eyes, wiped away her tears and headed into the next phase of her life, that of becoming a mother.

CHAPTER 7

Back at May's house goodbyes were said. There was sadness in being separated after such a short time of getting to know each other. This small family was brought together in their love for one man, now gone, leaving them to stay together in this world and go on without him. With the responsibility and sadness of Tom's funeral over with and the sun bright on this cold autumn day, Reeny began to feel the slightest thaw in her cold heart. She thought of the warm life growing in her, just below the iceberg of her heart. She knew then the warmth of the new life in her would melt the ice formed around her heart. With this growing hope she was able to put a tentative smile on her face and bid her sister-in-law goodbye, promising to write often and visit again soon. Although May had lost her brother, she was comforted knowing she and her girls had become part of this loving family. She felt blessed knowing that a part of Tom was growing in Reeny. In a way he would always be with them.

A few days after returning home from Tom's funeral, Frannie realized the little town of Oak Creek seemed different. Perhaps it was because she no longer felt like a naïve young teenager. She was forced to grow up in hurry. The sorrow of losing Tom weighed heavily on her family and was a palpable presence in their home. She tried not to resent the way her lovely sister was deserting her. Reeny withdrew from everyone. Even Mom was not allowed to enter Reeny's circle of sadness. Dad kept telling Mom and Frannie to give Reeny more time and slowly she would start to emerge from her grief. She needed more time to grieve. As the days grew into weeks, and it became colder and darker outside, the family began to worry about Reeny's noticeable mood changes. Mom attributed them to Reeny's early pregnancy. It scared Frannie to watch Reeny go off to work with Mom, seemingly happy and somewhat interested in the workday, only to return that same evening in a completely different mood. With downcast eyes Reeny would mumble to herself, refuse to eat any dinner, and take refuge in her bed well before nightfall.

"Reeny, please let me help you," Frannie begged as she sat on the edge of her sister's bed, stoking Reeny's tear stained face. In her distress over Reeny's silence and feeling shut out, Frannie went on rambling, "I'm not the little girl you think I am. I know what it's like to be a woman and to love a man. Don't shut me out, Reeny. I love you. I need you. I am your sister."

Slowly Reeny sat up in her bed and pulled her sweater tighter around her shoulders. She looked seriously at Frannie and said, "What are you talking about, Frannie? You're just a kid, only fifteen years old. You're just beginning to see how much fun high school will be. You haven't even started dating yet. What boys do you know, other than Janet's brother Tim, and to him, you're just one more girl in his family."

Their eyes met and Frannie could see that finally Reeny's attention was focusing on something other than her own great sorrow. Frannie was the first to look away. She lowered her eyes, nervously picking at the white tufts of cotton string hanging from the braided edge of the bedspread. Suddenly Reeny grabbed the material out of Frannie's twisting fingers. She grabbed Frannie's hands in her own and whispered harshly, "Look at me, Frannie! What did you mean when you said you know what it's like to love a man? Surely, you and Tim are just friends. Do you have a crush on Tim? That must be what you meant. You have a puppy love crush on Tim." This idea actually brought a half smile to Reeny's face as she said to Frannie, "Oh, Frannie, that is so sweet, your first crush on a boy. I will admit you picked a cutie pie. My lovely, baby sister, forgive me. I have been so wrapped up in my own misery, I haven't been able to give anyone else a single thought or care." It seemed like the sun had finally broken through the clouds that surrounded Reeny's face. Frannie was relieved to see some life and comprehension in Reeny's face. She could not bear to upset her sister with the truth, so she let her believe the simple, half-truths she had already guessed.

After that first intimate talk Reeny and Frannie began to reclaim the closeness they had before Tom entered their lives. Perhaps it was those first icy cold days of early winter, with its gloriously sunny but freezing cold days that helped them. Just having the brilliant northern sunshine for a few hours each day seemed to lift Reeny's spirits. She began to laugh again and slowly let herself feel happiness over the life growing within her. Perhaps she was afraid to love again. Perhaps it was too soon after Tom had been so swiftly and cruelly taken from her. But Frannie could see she was changing. She wasn't the cheery, starry-eyed young woman she was six months ago. This new Reeny was more mature, quieter, with a sly sense of humor well hidden until something funny struck her. It was like the innocent girl she had been before Tom's death was somewhere buried in this new mature women and that girl would slip out every now and then to reclaim a youthfulness that had been so swiftly stolen away from her. Reeny noticed changes in Frannie too. Frannie's heart was filled with newfound feelings of young love for Tim. To offset this wonderful new discovery had come her first experience of intense feelings of sorrow and loss caused by Tom's death. After experiencing the myriad of feelings she had been through in the last month, she could never be the innocent teenager she was when her family left her at the Slocums that fateful weekend they learned of Tom's death. Neither Reeny nor Frannie would ever be the same again. They had both grown up, sadly and quickly, like the rest of the world at this time.

Life went on. The world quickly realized it was time to bury the dead, rebuild devastated countries, and put millions of personal lives back together. With a collective sigh, humanity decided it was now time to wipe away a world of tears and get on with the business of living.

CHAPTER 8

Reeny and Mom went on with their work at the law firm. Dad found part-time work in a local accounting firm, and Frannie went on with high school. She and Janet were still very close friends, spending Friday nights together. That first time Frannie saw Tim after Tom's death, she felt different and much more grown up. If having her first sexual encounter had not forced some semblance of maturity on her, then the enormous sorrow experienced by Tom's death surely finalized her stepping into young adulthood. She was not the starry-eyed innocent fifteen-year-old she had been when she lost her virginity to Tim that early autumn afternoon. She still imagined herself in love with him. She loved seeing him whenever she stayed at Janet's house. She loved the way he would smile at her when no one else was watching. She loved the way he brushed up against her whenever they passed in the hallways at school. As things began to settle down that early winter, they were able to meet each other in quiet places, the edge of the meadow where they had sledded, the bookstore by the pot bellied wood stove. Places were they sat and held hands and talked about how the war had changed their small town. They talked about Reeny and how sad she was not to have Tom with her, especially now as she watched other young men come home from the war to be with their wives and sweethearts. They talked about Reeny's baby, what a blessing that she had something of Tom still with her. But they never talked about that afternoon in the Slocums' basement. It was as if they didn't know how to acknowledge it had happened. It was the first sexual experience for either of them and they didn't know how to express their thoughts about it in words. So instead, they basked in the happiness of just being together. They were not experienced enough to know how to make their relationship move forward, so, like all young people newly in love, they lived in the present, unshackled by any expectations of what they should be doing in a formal relationship. In their innocence, they simply enjoyed each other's company. Their love and friendship grew like a new bloom in spring, so fresh and eager. The people who knew them realized they were getting closer. With so many more important issues resulting from the war's end to occupy everyone's mind, Tim and Frannie were overlooked as young kids in puppy love.

One afternoon Tim and Frannie were walking across Old Farm Rd when he stopped suddenly, turned and said, "Frannie, I've been accepted at Northwestern on a scholarship. It's what I was working towards, what I have been praying for, and now it has come true. I will leave at the end of January, right after I graduate midterm. Frannie, I wanted to ask you if you would write to me, send me snapshots of yourself, maybe come up with my family sometimes to visit me. I know I can't ask you to be my girl. You're too young for that and besides, I won't be here to take you to the school football games or dances or junior prom or any of that stuff. But I like you a lot, Frannie, and it would mean so much to me if I knew you were thinking of me while I was up at Northwestern. I'll be thinking of you whenever I'm not swamped with homework or playing sports."

Frannie's heart felt like it would burst in her chest, it felt so tight. Tim was leaving her. He was going away to college. She wouldn't see him at school everyday after this semester. He wouldn't be at the Slocums when she went there to spend the weekend with Janet. She couldn't let him see how hurt she was. This was his big chance. He needed this scholarship. The Slocums had so many kids they couldn't ever pay for Tim to go to college, and he was their only son. Everyone adored Tim and wanted him to have this chance to go to Northwestern. He deserved it and Frannie would not ruin it for him. She would not make him sad that he was going away. She swallowed the lump in her throat, took a deep breath and said, "Congratulations, Tim, I'm so happy for you and I'm so proud of you. You know I will write, all the time in fact. You'll get so many letters from me you can give them away to any lonely guys up there who have no one to write to them. I'll flood that college with letters to you. And pictures, you know I'm getting a Kodak box camera for Christmas. You better have a whole wall in your dorm room for my pictures." Then suddenly, so he wouldn't see the tears forming in her eyes, she threw her arms around his neck, brought his face down to hers and kissed him long and hard. Their kiss was warm and sweet and quickly grew passionate. They both realized the joy they had found in each other would soon be gone. They instinctively knew their future held the hurt of separation for both of them. As they pulled apart slowly, Frannie heard Tim whisper in her ear, "I love you, Frannie," and she whispered back her love for him as they walked, arm in arm, back to her house.

That weekend was damp and cold. The snow was slushy and the roads were slippery. The sun was hidden behind a sky full of dark, wet clouds. It was depressing weather and Frannie and Reeny had been cooped up in the house all weekend. Frannie was unusually quiet, staying in their room reading and working on her schoolwork. Reeny looked up from the novel she was reading while laying on her bed and noticed Frannie was looking at the wall calender with a frown on her face. Everyone had heard of Tim's scholarship and the whole town knew he would be leaving after midterm graduation in January. Reeny figured Frannie was counting the time she had left with Tim. She closed her book, got out of her bed and went over to Frannie and said, "Don't be too sad, Frannie. This is Tim's big chance. You'll still see him. You can go with his family to visit him, and I'm sure he'll come back to town once in a while for visits."

Frannie turned towards her older sister and looked into her eyes. Reeny could see she was very puzzled as she said, "That's not what I'm thinking about, Reeny. I'm checking the calendar to count days. So much has been happening in the last few weeks that I didn't think about it until now. I haven't gotten my menstruation for this month. I am three weeks late."

Reeny's first thought was Frannie must be off schedule. She had been through so many emotional upheavals in such a short time. Then she remembered the conversation she and Frannie had a short while ago. She recalled Frannie saying something about knowing what it was like to love a man. She had assumed it meant nothing more than platonic, puppy love feelings towards Frannie's best friend's brother. Reeny looked into Frannie's confused and weary eyes. She began to feel a fear growing in her chest. She lifted Frannie's head with her hand as she sat down beside her on the bed. "Frannie, listen closely to me," she said, as she peered deeply and seriously into Frannie's eyes. "Are you still a virgin? Tell me the truth, Frannie, it's very important."

Frannie's eyes welled with tears as she tried to pull her face out of Reeny's hands. Looking down at her bed, her tears beginning to drop onto the bedspread, she said softly, "No, Reeny, I gave my virginity to Tim the weekend we learned Tom was dead. I didn't know about Tom when I was with Tim. We were alone together at the Slocums. Mr. and Mrs. Slocum and all the girls had gone into the city to get new clothes. Tim and I stayed behind. We went sledding and he kissed me. When we got back to the house we listened to the radio in the basement. We danced and then we kissed and then somehow we were together on the davenport. Before I could think very much about what was happening, I gave myself to Tim." Frannie was crying softly, her head resting on Reeny's shoulder as she went on, "Reeny, Tim didn't try to force me. He would never be that way. It just felt right. Everything about the entire day felt right. We were alone in the house. Everything we did that day brought us closer to each other. We ended up kissing on the davenport and I didn't think anymore. I just let my feelings take over and then suddenly we were undressed and I had given my virginity to Tim. Oh, Reeny, it was just that one time. We both promised not to let it happen again until we were older and married. Tim didn't think I would get pregnant since we only did it one time. I swear, Reeny, it only happened once. Tim is the most wonderful guy I've ever known. He would never hurt me on purpose. Reeny, I can't be pregnant. I'm too young even to be married. Why haven't I gotten my period yet? I always have it the same time each month. We have been through so many sad times. Do you think I haven't gotten my period because I've been so sad lately?" asked Frannie so innocently it made Reeny cry. Her baby sister was so young and naïve, so trusting of everyone, including Tim.

For a moment Reeny wanted to go to Tim and beat him until her fists were sore. Right now she hated him for what he had done to her sister. Even though Frannie admitted to being a willing partner, it infuriated Reeny. Tim was older and should know better. How dare he take advantage of her innocent, trusting sister who was barely out of her childhood. She believed Frannie when she told her Tim had been a virgin also. That did not excuse his behavior. He was older and guys talked a lot about sex. He should have known not to let his sexual feelings get beyond his control. Now the repercussions of that rash, impulsive act may have far reaching consequences, far more than Frannie could begin to imagine. She was too young and inexperienced to comprehend the trouble she may have gotten herself into.

As Reeny sat there on the bed trying to comfort and explain the situation to her younger sister, she did not have any idea what to do next. Her gut feeling was to take Frannie downstairs and tell Mom and Dad what had happened so they could figure out what to do. She knew they would be shocked. To them Frannie was still a little girl. She doubted they even acknowledged Frannie had entered puberty. She knew Mom was forced to, as she had to deal with Frannie starting her period and providing the necessary sanitary items each month. Other than that, she knew neither of her parents realized Frannie was a blossoming young woman. Reeny was confused for a moment. She could see the fear building up in Frannie's eyes. She heard it in her voice when Frannie said, "Reeny, I can see in your face you are worried. You think I'm pregnant, don't you? I can't believe that. It was only one time and it all happened so fast. How could a baby come from that?"

Reeny put her arms around Frannie's shoulders and pulled her close as she whispered in her ear, "Yes, Frannie, a baby could happen, even from one time. We have to tell Mom and Dad so they can figure out what to do."

Frannie jerked back, fear showing on her face as she cried out,

"No, no, Reeny, please don't say anything to them. Dad will be so mad at Tim. Mom will be ashamed of me. Please, Reeny, I don't want to tell them I'm not a virgin. They will think I'm a dirty person, having sex and not being married. Please, can't you help me, just you and me?" Reeny considered the situation more calmly. The initial shock was over and she realized it might be better if she and Frannie found out for sure whether Frannie was pregnant before they told Mom and Dad anything.

The two sisters talked late into the night, forming their plan. Reeny would take Frannie into Albany, the nearest big city, twenty miles north of Oak Creek. She would find a doctor and Frannie would act like she was Reeny, using her married name of Reeny St. Clair and wearing Reeny's still shiny wedding band. Reeny would leave the law office just after she arrived there with Mom, telling Mom she was sick and had to go home. They could drive up to Albany, see the doctor, and be back in time to pick Mom up by 5 p.m. They made their plans that night and went to bed satisfied this was the best solution for the time being.

CHAPTER 9

Early Monday morning Reeny called a doctor in Albany and made the appointment for the next morning. She would have to put a lot of Max Factor pancake makeup on Frannie to make her look older. They would manage it. They had to find out if Frannie was pregnant so she could figure out what to do next. If God was forgiving and generous, perhaps Frannie did just have a case of nerves. As planned, Reeny dropped Mom off at work, feigned illness and returned home to pick up Frannie. They drove up to Albany where Frannie saw the doctor who examined her while Reeny waited nervously in the waiting area. After being examined Frannie dressed and waited for the nurse to come and escort her back to Reeny. Instead, the nurse asked her to join Reeny and the doctor in his office. Together she and Reeny sat stiffly before the doctor, who somberly confirmed Reeny's suspicions. Frannie was pregnant, about two months along. Reeny's heart ached. Here she was just over three months pregnant herself. She was a widow, alone with no husband, leaning on her family for support and guidance. Now her younger sister was pregnant. Frannie was not mature enough to fully understand what sex encompassed. Frannie was not able to comprehend the enormity of situation she was in. Tom was dead and Tim was leaving soon to go away to college. There was no man in either of their lives to accept the responsibility of these babies or be emotionally or financially supportive to these young mothers. This would be a huge burden to place on their parents, but they had nowhere else to turn.

As Frannie sat there in stunned silence, Reeny thanked the doctor for his time and paid him for his services. Taking Frannie by the arm, Reeny guided her out of the doctor's office and placed her in the front seat of Dad's Buick. They drove about 20 minutes before either of them spoke. Frannie turned her face to Reeny and in a dazed voice said, "Reeny, I'm afraid. Mom and Dad will be so mad at me. Dad will kill Tim. He will think this is all Tim's fault. Reeny, I can't let Dad hurt Tim. He didn't mean for me to get pregnant. I don't even want Tim to know about the baby. He won't go away to Northwestern if he knows I'm pregnant. Reeny, Tim has to go to Northwestern. He has his scholarship. It's the only way he can pay for his college education. You know the Slocums don't have any extra money to send Tim to college. Please, Reeny, promise me you won't let Tim find out about the baby. Don't let Dad tell him. We can tell him later, after he's enrolled at Northwestern. I can quit school and get a job. I'll think of something. I just don't want Tim to know."

She was getting hysterical so Reeny tried to calm her down by saying, "Frannie, let me think. I'll come up with a plan. But we have to tell Mom and Dad. We are both going to need their help."

Reeny dropped Frannie off at the house, running in quickly to change her clothes and mess up her hair so she would look sick when she picked up Mom at the law office. It was nearly 5 p.m., so she wiped off her lipstick and headed out the door. When they returned home, Mom walked into the house looking tired, followed by Reeny feigning sickness. Reeny chose this moment to head upstairs, leaving Frannie alone to watch her tired mother take off her coat and hat, lay it on the dinette chair and head over to the stove to start dinner. "Where's your dad, Frannie? Has he called? Maybe he's working late tonight," she mumbled more to herself than to Frannie.

"I don't know, Mom" was all Frannie could say. Mom barely noticed Frannie's distant manner. Frannie just sat at the dinette staring at her hands. As pots and pans clanged together, the noise finally penetrated Frannie's consciousness. She got up and started setting the table.

Just as Frannie finished setting the table for dinner, her father walked into the house. Grabbing his wife around the waist, he placed a kiss on her neck, hugging her and lifting her up off her feet a couple inches. After putting her safely back on the ground in front of the stove, Dad grabbed Frannie next. He hugged his young daughter, asking her, "How's my little girl? How was school today?" Frannie felt so ashamed. She would never be her dad's little girl again. She would have to lie to him and pretend she was at school today when she was really at the doctor's getting news that would turn everyone's world upside down. With her limited experience of life's complications, she could not figure out how her life had changed so drastically and so suddenly. Instinct told her she better grow up fast and pay attention to life because her world was going to quickly change even more. Because of what she had done, her family's life was going to be altered. She had no idea of what the future held for her. In her short span of living she could not picture the distant future. She could not comprehend the impending outcome resulting from her past actions. All she could do in her youth and inexperience was wait for her parents to find out she was pregnant and tell her what she was supposed to do. She could not figure out how to tell her parents about her dilemma. She had been her family's baby for fifteen years. She did not know how to handle something as complicated as having her own baby. She could only wait for Reeny to come downstairs and take care of telling Mom and Dad the shameful news of what she had done. That was as far ahead as she could think, so she continued to sit silently at the kitchen table.

Finally, Mom finished cooking dinner and the family gathered together to eat. It was quiet around the dinner table that evening. Mom and Dad were tired from their day at work. Reeny and Frannie were quiet with their secret. Reeny knew Frannie depended on her to figure out how to tell Mom and Dad that Frannie was pregnant. Earlier, while upstairs by herself, Reeny found herself becoming very angry with Frannie. Reeny could not believe Frannie had behaved in such an irresponsible way. Then she got mad at Mom and Dad. They ignored Frannie's growing up into a young woman. Obviously, Mom hadn't explained much about conception to Frannie. They hadn't wanted to admit their younger daughter was becoming a woman, and now the entire family would pay the price, especially Frannie. Reeny knew she had to speak now, no matter how tired everyone was. She could not go to bed with the secret still untold. She did not want to wake up tomorrow morning with this burden. She did not want to be the only one trying to figure out a solution to this new problem. She and Frannie needed their parents' help. Lifting her head, she caught Frannie's eye. The two sisters exchanged sad but determined glances.

"Mom, Dad," began Reeny in a soft voice, "Frannie and I must talk to you. We must tell you something very important." Mom and Dad looked at both their girls, then at each other, and braced for news they felt would not be good. With no softening preamble, Reeny bluntly said, "Frannie is pregnant." It was out. Now it was up to Frannie to follow with her explanation. Both parents gasped. Color drained out of their tired faces and all eyes shifted to Frannie.

"That's impossible," said Mom. "She's just a little girl."

With sad eyes Dad looked at Frannie. He realized, perhaps for the first time, that she was not a little girl anymore. He looked puzzled. When had his Frannie grown into a woman? It seemed like only yesterday she was a little girl jumping rope and crying over scraped knees. But no, it wasn't really yesterday. It was years ago. While the world went crazy fighting a war, his Frannie had gown up. He had barely taken the time to notice his little girl had grown into a woman. Now, as life settled down and he had time to look, it was too late. His Frannie had been robbed of her youth, first by the war and now by a baby coming into her life too soon. He felt old beyond his years. He had failed his daughters. He should have been able to protect them. It was his job to shield them both from hurt. He was their father, the man who had given them life. He was supposed to take care of them. Consumed with his feelings of failure, he did not notice a tear slip down is cheek. He felt his wife's arm around his shoulders as he heard her saying, "Stan, Stan, please answer me. You're scaring us. You're not hearing anything Frannie is saying." He looked over at Frannie. What could his young daughter say to him that would assuage his guilt over not protecting her from harm? Frannie was crying and begging him not to tell Tim. Somehow the fact that there was a father for this baby had never entered his mind, so shocked was he by the news of Frannie's pregnancy.

"Tim, you mean Tim Slocum," he answered dumbly, still too

shocked to accept that his virgin daughter had been intimate with a boy. It was obvious she had been and now it had to be dealt with. "Tim is just a boy. He's going away to college. He's too young to be a father," said Stan, as if that would solve the problem at hand.

"Stan, you're not making any sense," said Mom. Stella realized Stan was still dazed from the news and she would have to take the helm for now.

"Of course he's not old enough to be a father, and neither is Frannie old enough to be a mother. But they were both old enough to have sex and make this baby. Now we have to figure out what we are going to do. Frannie needs us to be strong. So does Reeny. We are a family, Stan. We will work this out." Stella turned a piercing look on her two daughters and said, "For now, the news stays in this family until your dad and I have figured out what to do." Assured by quiet nods from everyone around the table, she continued more calmly as she said, "Now let's finish dinner, clean the kitchen and all of us get to bed before we drop. We will all think more clearly after we get some sleep." Summoning all the strength she had left in her body, she got up from the table and began clearing away the dishes.

Freezing cold temperatures met them all as they were leaving the house the following morning. The four of them drove off in the Buick. Reeny was driving. She was dropping Frannie off at school, Dad at the accounting office and she and Mom were going on to the law firm. There was none of their usual chitchat in the car this morning. The news of Frannie's pregnancy was foremost on everyone's mind. As Reeny maneuvered the Buick up next to the curb, careful to watch out for high school kids crossing in every direction, she saw Tim walking towards them. It was obvious Tim was waiting to meet Frannie and walk her to class. She could see Dad looking down at his hands, afraid to trust himself to see Tim. Frannie quickly got out of the back seat and ran off towards the building, anxious to get away from Dad. Watching Frannie's face glow as she looked up at Tim, it didn't seem possible their world had just been turned upside down. Just from watching these two happy teenagers, no one would guess there was such a problem brewing with far reaching consequences that would affect them both for the rest of their lives.

"Gosh, Frannie, you look great. Your cheeks are so pink, and darn, your eyes are so sparkly," gushed Tim, as Frannie ran breathlessly up to him walking to class.

"I'm just so happy to see you, Tim," replied Frannie, as she smiled up at him. She loved walking with him at school. All the girls looked their way, smiling at her and Tim. She knew they made an attractive couple and she basked in the admiration of the other students, proud they thought of her as Tim's girl. It was almost impossible to think she had a baby growing inside her. It was so much fun being here at school with Tim, going to her classes, talking to her girlfriends, and planning the semester's events. Homecoming was just a few weeks away. Tim was the captain of the football team, so he was busy with practicing after school for the big game. Frannie was busy with her girlfriends. She spent her spare time planning the homecoming dance with Janet and her other school friends. Most of the time she was so caught up with her classes and her social activities, she didn't even remember she was carrying a baby. She decided not to worry about it until after Tim went away to Northwestern. From now until he graduated in January, they had lots of time to be together and lots of fun things to do. She didn't want to spoil his last days in high school. Besides, after he left for Northwestern she would have plenty of time to think about the baby and what she would do. She had gotten pregnant that one night in October, so no one would be able to tell she was pregnant for a long time. She was comforted thinking Reeny would help her. Reeny would think of a plan, she always did. In her childish way she imagined she and Reeny would go on living with Mom and Dad and eventually there would be two babies for them to play with. Her youth and immaturity did not allow her to think logically about her future.

The intensity of the winter chill crept over the small Midwestern town of Oak Creek as Thanksgiving approached. Oak Creek High won the homecoming game with Frannie and her family screaming neck in neck with all the Slocums and the rest of Tim's fan club of students. Even Reeny was caught up in the excitement and joy of the evening. For a few hours that evening she was able to forget about her constantly aching heart and enjoy life with her family and friends. By now most of the town knew Reeny's tragic story. She was the young war widow who had recently buried her heroic husband and now must go on to raise her fatherless child. She had the sympathy and support of the townspeople. Tom was not from Oak Creek, but he was a fallen soldier and everyone's hero. Reeny was their hometown girl. The town rallied around her and her family to help ease the pain of their loss. Shouts of hello and good natured ribbing were heard all over the school bleachers. Classmates were teasing Frannie about her football player boyfriend. Waves and hello's greeted Reeny, Frannie, and their parents as they searched out a seat next to the noisy, cheering Slocums. For a brief time Stan McFadden was able to forget his worries about his two daughters as he got caught up in the excitement of the football game.

Stan McFadden was an honest, hardworking man of his word. He lived a decent, truthful life. He was kind, responsible, and always available to help wherever and whenever he was needed. It did not sit well with his principles, this cover-up he was maintaining at Frannie's request. Rather than dwell on the unfairness of what life had dealt him and his two daughters, Stan was a man of action. When he encountered a problem, he searched for and found a solution. He put that solution into action and solved his problems. For the first time in Stan's life, he was faced with a problem he could not solve. For once he had to step back and consider someone else's solution to a problem he could not remedy singlehandedly. This deceit, this keeping Frannie's pregnancy a secret from the Slocums, did not sit well with Stan's conscience. But Frannie was adamant, desperate that Tim not be told about her pregnancy. Frannie had made this decision and was fierce in her determination that nothing would keep Tim from going away to Northwestern. So, for the time being, Stan chewed the bitter straw of deceit and kept his feelings to himself. It changed him. He could not socialize and talk easily with Mel

Slocum, knowing the secret he kept from this decent man who loved his own family and who also included Frannie in his heart. Stan knew in his heart Mel had a right to know he would be a grandfather. But Frannie had demanded his secrecy and his first allegiance was to his daughter. Stan pacified himself with the knowledge that eventually the Slocums would be told about the baby. He expected Frannie to remain at home while Tim continued at Northwestern. He assumed once Tim was enrolled at the university and well into his class schedule he would not want to quit. Stan was willing to help Tim and Frannie in any way he could. He did think Tim would marry Frannie. He would demand that much as soon as their secret was out. He could handle the town gossip about a shotgun wedding, but an illegitimate baby was out of the question. So for now, he held his tongue and kept the secret against his better judgement. He hoped someday in the future his friend Mel Slocum would understand and forgive him his deceit.

CHAPTER 10

Thanksgiving and Christmas came and went while the bitter cold of a Midwestern winter settled on the small town of Oak Creek. The Slocums and the McFaddens became closer friends as Tim and Frannie's relationship deepened and the time for Tim's departure drew near. Even Reeny was pulled into the circle of these two loving families. Naturally slim, Reeny's pregnancy barely showed even after four months. Her's was the pregnancy everyone knew about and talked about and planned for. It was easy for Frannie to forget about her own pregnancy as all attention was shifted to Reeny and the baby due late in May or early June. Reeny and Mom continued working at the law firm while Dad was immersed in his accounting practice. He had started working part-time while the war was winding down. Now with the young men coming home, getting jobs, and starting families, his services for loans and investment counseling were in demand. As the new year approached, things were settling down into a routine at the McFaddens, at least for the time being. No one was quite sure how the coming year would play out with all the loose ends hanging.

Early in January, Reeny came home from work early one afternoon. Mom stayed behind, promised a ride home later from one of the partners. Thinking she had eaten something that made her sick, Reeny laid down on her bed, trying to calm the nausea and cramping she was feeling. She dozed uneasily in the quiet of the dim house. Drifting in and out of sleep, she was haunted by visions of Tom's face. At times as she lay in this half sleep she was comforted with the feeling of being very close to him. She could almost feel him. He was so real to her in this dream state she vacillated within. As she drifted deeper asleep she wanted to be closer to him, to feel his arms holding her as she fell asleep. Dreaming of Tom, she finally fell into a deep slumber. Several hours later she was jolted awake by sharp, searing pains in her abdomen. The house was dark. No one was home yet. The pain was overwhelming. She could barely sit up. She cried out in the empty house. She reached over but the pain prevented her from moving far enough to reach the bedside lamp. All she could do was lay there in agonizing pain. As the pain continued, she felt wetness between her legs, as if she had started her period. But this was not like an ordinary menstrual flow. The wetness and the flow was spreading fast, soppy her clothing and the bedding she lay in. She was afraid. Slowly it dawned on her that she was having a miscarriage. She could feel the life she carried in her womb being expelled onto the bed. She could feel the agonizing cramping of that expulsion. She could feel the flowing and the wetness of fluid as the contents of her womb spilled onto the sheets between her legs. The pain she felt in her abdomen did not compare to the pain in her heart as she began to comprehend what was happening. She knew she was too weak and in too much pain to do anything about her predicament. With the terrible ache in her heart growing as fast as she was losing her baby, she calmly decided she didn't want to live without her child. She laid her head down, gritted her teeth and begged God's mercy in her suffering. She did not care about living anymore. She was ready to go with her child to be with Tom in Heaven. She decided that was where they would be a family.

Frannie was the first one home. She was confused. The Buick was in the garage but no lights were on in the house. Where were Mom and Reeny? They should both be at work. Frannie wondered why the Buick was home. The house was dark and quiet as Frannie ran up the stairs to see if Reeny was in their bedroom. As she flew open the bedroom door, she switched on the light chain and gasped as she saw Reeny lying in a pool of blood soaking her white eyelet bedspread. She grabbed Reeny's shoulders, shaking her, talking to her. Reeny was incoherent, mumbling something about seeing Tom. Frannie ran back downstairs, grabbed the telephone and frantically called Dad. As she ran back upstairs to help Reeny, she quickly grabbed towels from the bathroom. Once inside their bedroom she threw off Reeny's bedspread and stuffed rolled towels between Reeny's legs to stem the flow of blood. Within minutes Dad arrived from his office. After running upstairs and immediately recognizing the urgency of the situation, he and Frannie managed to wrap Reeny in towels and a blanket. He grabbed his bleeding daughter and carried her downstairs. He gently placed a semi-conscious Reeny in the backseat of the Buick as Frannie quickly got in beside her. With his heart beating too fast, he drove at a reckless speed the five miles to Community Hospital. Reeny was admitted and taken to her room while the doctor was called in to tend to her. Mom walked into the waiting room just a few minutes after Reeny was taken to a room. Dad had called her from his office just after Frannie had called him. For the next two hours the three of them paced the floor of the waiting room, wondering with heavy hearts what the doctor would tell them. Just as they began to hear the roll of the hospital dinner carts, the doctor came to talk to them. With a somber look on his face, he delivered the news they were sadly expecting. "Reeny had a miscarriage. She will be all right. She is sleeping now. I've given her a sedative and she will sleep all night. She is young and she will be able to have other children. I'm sorry. I will be back in the morning to check on her." The doctor did not mince his words. He delivered his news, silently grieving with this family, but went on with his business of healing others. His services were always in demand and he had others to care for. He walked away, down the long corridor, leaving this family to mourn the loss of their unborn child.

Mom, Dad, and Frannie sat down on the cold Naugahyde of the waiting room couch. They were stunned and silent. Finally, Frannie lifted her head and looked at her mother and father as she said, "I am so sorry Reeny has lost her baby. It doesn't seem possible. Reeny is so good, so kind to everyone. She doesn't deserve this. She just lost Tom and now she has lost her baby too. I am the one who should have lost a baby. I'm not even married. I don't want my baby the way Reeny wanted her and Tom's baby. Tim doesn't even know about our baby. I'm too young for this baby, and I don't want Tim's scholarship ruined because of our baby. Oh, Mom, Dad, I wish it were me, not Reeny, who lost her baby. It's not fair." Frannie broke down and sobbed into her mother's arms.

At that moment Stan and Stella's eyes met for a moment over their young daughter's head. Without wanting to put such outrageous thoughts into words, both parents were thinking this might be a solution to Frannie's problem. Finally, Stan could not be silent. The stakes were too high. His thoughts had to be voiced. "Stella, you know we have not faced what we are going to do about Frannie's pregnancy. I have not thought sensibly about the future since Frannie begged me to be silent until a plan could be formulated. Now this terrible thing has happened to Reeny. Please forgive me, Stella, but I can't help thinking maybe this will help us out of our dilemma with Frannie. I may be crazy, but it sounds like Frannie would like to go on with her life unencumbered with a child at her young age. She's made it perfectly clear she does not want Tim burdened with the child she is carrying. I know this sounds shocking, but I will be honest. I am thinking this is a way Frannie can have her baby with no one knowing about its illegitimacy, and Reeny can still have a child to love. I know it won't be hers and Tom's child, but it will be her own sister's child. No one but our family ever needs to know about this." Stan finished speaking, looking at his wife and younger daughter.

Stella looked stunned and said quietly, "Are you saying we should not let anyone know about Reeny's miscarriage, send the girls off somewhere until Frannie has her baby, and let them return together as if the baby was Reeny's child?"

"Yes," answered Stan, "that is what I am suggesting. If Reeny will accept it, I think it would be the best thing for our family. We have lost one baby tonight. I want the losing to stop in my family. I can't bear anymore. We have lost Tom, now we have lost his child. Thank God we did not lose our Reeny. We have our girls and we have Frannie's baby." Stan turned to look at Frannie as he said very seriously, "If Reeny agrees to accept your child as her own, is that what you want, Frannie?"

Frannie replied quickly, "Yes, Dad, if Reeny can accept my baby as her own, I think that would be a good way to work all this out. I am so sorry for what I have done to you and Mom and to Tim. If Reeny will take my baby, I can go on with my life and not feel guilty about having this baby. I know Reeny will love it and care for it much better than I could ever do. I am too young to have a baby to care for. Yes, Dad, please ask Reeny about this idea. I don't want to keep worrying about my baby. Sometimes I even pretend it doesn't exist. If only Reeny will say yes. I can stop worrying about everything."

As Stan saw the relief on his daughter's face, he suddenly realized how young she was. With a sadness deep in his heart he realized Frannie had kept all the worry about her baby bottled up inside herself. Yes, this did seem like a solution, if only Reeny could get past her grief and see it this way also.

The next day was clear and cold. The sun shone high in the sky but no warmth reached the earth and it did not get above ten degrees. Frannie was wrapped in a warm woolen coat as she trudged over the crunchy ice with Janet heading to their next class. Tim caught up with them, his breath coming out in white puffs. "Hey, ladies, you better hurry or you'll be late to class. Frannie, where were you last night? I came by your house but no one was home. I thought we could take a ride. Dad let me have the truck to run an errand. Did you go somewhere with your family?" asked Tim, concern showing in his sincere face.

As she saw the concern for her and her family in Tim's eyes, she hated lying to him, but she had no choice. Janet was standing right next to her, so she could only answer vaguely, "Yes, Tim, we had some shopping to do. Dad took us all together and then we stopped at the diner and had a bite to eat." Tim looked relieved as he smiled and waved goodbye to Frannie and Janet. He was in a hurry to get to his class. Finals were next week. After that he would be done with high school. He would graduate midterm as he had planned. After packing his clothes and spending some time with his family, he would drive up to Northwestern the last week of January.

As Frannie and Janet walked to their class, Janet noticed the change in Frannie's mood. "What's the matter, Frannie? You seem like you're not here today. You look distracted and you barely talked to Tim. Don't you like him anymore? You seem to be avoiding my whole family. Are you mad at us?" asked Janet, almost on the verge of tears. Janet loved Frannie and her family. Janet felt so sorry for Reeny. Reeny had suffered so much sorrow and loss for such a young woman. Janet didn't want to lose Frannie as her best friend.

Frannie was quick to reassure her friend of her love and loyalty as she said, "I'm sorry, Janet. I love you and your family. You are like a sister to me. It's just that I've been so concerned about Reeny. She misses Tom so much. She has to be careful not to get depressed. I'm glad she has the new baby coming to help cheer her up." Frannie felt so deceitful and was ashamed of herself as the lies slipped so easily from her lips. It was important to keep up the pretense of Reeny's continued pregnancy. Everyone in town must continue to think Reeny was carrying Tom's child.

Arm in arm, the two friends continued across the campus, going to their classes. Frannie didn't dare let on to Janet anything about the baby of Tim's she was carrying. After last night, even though her family had suffered a terrible loss, she felt relieved for herself. Finally there was a possible solution to the problem she had kept hidden for the last three months. Semester end was coming up soon. Tim would leave for Northwestern and she could begin to plan with her family what to do about her unborn child. She prayed Reeny would agree with the plan Mom and Dad had talked to her about. They were at the hospital now, talking to Reeny and making plans for both of their daughters. Now it all depended on Reeny and whether she would accept Frannie's baby as her own. Frannie prayed Reeny would let her baby replace the one her sister had just lost. Frannie prayed her sister loved her enough to help her in this desperate time. She prayed silently as she and Janet went into the warm classroom, praying her sister would become the mother her child needed for the future.

With Tim and Janet reassured of her love and friendship, Frannie walked home later that afternoon with a lighter heart than she had since learning she was pregnant. The Buick was in the driveway and Dad's new truck was parked behind it. She walked into the house and saw Mom and Dad sitting at the table. Neither one had gone to work today, as they were tending to Reeny and getting her home from the hospital. Dad had spoken to the doctor, begging for his silence and explaining they wished to spare Reeny any reminders of this sorrowful event. They were thankful Doc Darnel was old and ready to retire soon. The whole town knew he planned on retiring and moving down to Oklahoma to be near his daughter and her family. He would be gone by the time Frannie and Reeny came home with the baby they planned to have everyone believe was Reeny's. The three of them sat down at the table, as Dad told Frannie he had explained their plan to Reeny. Dad told them both how Reeny was so hurt and sad, but when he began to ask for her help in taking Frannie's baby as her own, her eyes began to shine and the tears stopped. She had looked unbelievingly at Dad and had not hesitated a moment before answering him. Reeny had told Dad she thought her life was over, with the loss of Tom and then her baby being too much for her to bear. She never imagined Frannie was so afraid of having her baby. She thought it was a miracle that her family wanted her to be the mother of Frannie's baby. She felt like she was being given a second chance at life. She wanted Frannie's baby with her whole heart. Dad had brought Reeny home from the hospital that same morning. He did not want to bring any extra attention to her being there. Hospital records were confidential. Dad had impressed on Doctor Darnel the confidentiality of his daughter's ordeal. He felt sure the doctor had acted alone in filling out necessary paperwork. They hoped the staff's memory of that day would be short and soon forgotten.

CHAPTER 11

It was an emotional day when Tim left for Northwestern. The train station was crowded with the Slocums and the McFaddens gathered around Tim. Everyone was crying and hugging Tim and wishing him well. Frannie felt totally withdrawn. Her plans for the future, for her and her child, were already decided. She had to get through this scene of saying goodbye to Tim. She was being an actress, pretending to be happy. Frannie acted like their separation was short lived, making sure Tim believed they would see each other at spring break only a few months away. She would not do anything to spoil his moment of finally getting out of this town and going away to college. His leaving was the key to his future and she would not stand in his way, not her or this child. Thanks to Dad, Mom, and Reeny, she was being given a second chance. Her baby would be loved and mothered by Reeny. She would always have the child in her life. She would be her baby's aunt. That was enough for her. She felt lucky to have some part in her child's life. She could not be her child's mother. She was too young and could not do that job. But she would still have the child near her. She would love this child as an aunt and that much she could handle. Never once did she feel she was cheating Tim. In her young mind she made the decision to give Tim his college education over his own child. She knew in her heart her decision was not just for Tim. It was for herself. She could not handle motherhood at this point in her life, with or without Tim. She was too young and naïve to feel guilty for not giving Tim the opportunity to make the decision himself about fatherhood. Believing she was doing what was best for both of them, she made her decision and was relieved by it. Tim was leaving to begin the next phase of his life, and she was ready to do the same.

The start of the year saw many new beginnings in Oak Creek. Tim went up to Northwestern to start his new beginning at the university.

For awhile Reeny went back to work and Frannie went back to school. For these sisters, this was a temporary existence. Their new beginning was shortly delayed as Mom and Dad planned for the future. With Tim gone away to Northwestern and Tom buried up near May's home, the McFaddens began to take stock of their ties to Oak Creek. Obviously, the two sisters must move away, even if only temporarily. Mom had a sister in California. Reeny and Frannie could go and live with their aunt and uncle in Pasadena. As Stan and Stella talked about the girls leaving, the more it made sense for all of them to move out west. Stan was semi-retired. He was an accountant. There was plenty of opportunity out west with so many young people heading to the sunny state to make their fortunes. Mom was ready to go. Her sister lived in California and she was always trying to entice Mom to move closer to her. For years Mom's sister had tried coaxing Mom to move to the sunny state where the warm weather was good for everyone's health. Mom's sister, Lilian, had tried to convince Stan and Stella to move out of the bitter Midwestern cold. Lillian constantly wrote to them how the warm weather would help Stella's arthritis. Now there did not seem any reason for the McFadden family to split up, especially with the new baby coming in the summer. When all the pros and cons were discussed, the family decided to move out west.

Stan put the house up for sale while Mom wrote long letters to Lillian seeking her help in finding a home for the McFaddens to rent until they could find more permanent housing. Mom knew she would have to let Lillian know the truth about the girls' babies, but she decided it was news she wanted to talk about in person. She would wait until they all arrived in California before giving Lillian the sad news about Reeny's miscarriage and their plan for Reeny to become mother to Frannie's unborn child. Thus far, no one except Stan, Stella, and Reeny knew about Frannie's pregnancy.

Stan hoped the house would sell soon. The family could not afford to take a loss financially on the sale of their home. They needed the profit to start new in California. They could not remain in Oak Creek for much longer. People would begin to notice Reeny was not getting bigger in her supposed pregnancy, and Frannie's pregnancy couldn't be hidden for much longer. Stan was anxious to get his family out west. He felt confident this would be the best thing for all his womenfolk who had suffered so much this past year. The bright sunshine of California would cheer Reeny up and make her forget the sorrowful loss of her husband and baby. Yes, Stan reasoned, it was time to put the sorrow of this past year behind them and seek out a new beginning in the sunny orange groves of southern California. He was thankful Lillian was so welcoming and anxious to have them all move closer to her. Stan had spent his whole life here in the Midwest, yet he had no dread of leaving here. He was an adventurous man. Having lived through the depression and a world war, he figured there wasn't a lot of hardship or sadness he hadn't already encountered. All that mattered to him now was his girls' happiness and the safety and future of them and his unborn grandchild. If moving west meant their happiness then that's where they'd all move. He was getting excited. He wanted a fresh start in California. He had a comfortable monthly sum from his retirement savings, and with the money from selling their house, he figured they'd be solvent until he found work in California. His accounting background would enable him to find a job that paid decent enough for him to take care of his family. He had heard talk about California booming, especially southern California. Movies were the big excitement with the war's end. The young men had returned from the war and were looking for entertainment. Hollywood was the country's new Mecca, beckoning swarms of young, talented men and women to make their fortunes out west in the movie industry. These people would need Stan's investment guidance. Stan was confident it was a good move. So with this reassuring attitude, Stan prepared his family for the move to California.

Frannie knew she had to face her best friend, Janet, and the rest of the Slocum family to prepare them for her departure. She felt sneaky and unworthy of the Slocums' love and trust in her. She knew she was running away and taking Tim's child away from this wonderful family who had accepted her and loved her unconditionally. With a heavy heart Frannie trudged slowly out to the Slocums' farmhouse.

Janet was crying as she and Frannie sat on her bed. Frannie tried to comfort her best friend as she said, "Janet, please try to understand, I have to move. My family is going to California. I am so excited. I love thinking about living where the sun shines all the time and living so close to where they are making movies. I'll go to a big high school with lots of kids, and it never gets cold or snows there. I think it's wonderful. The only bad thing is leaving you and moving so far away from Tim. But, Janet, be honest. You know Tim is going to be busy making the good grades he needs to keep his scholarship. He won't have much time to come home. I don't want him feeling like he has to think of me when he should be concentrating on making good grades."

Frannie was amazed that her feelings for Tim seemed so uncomplicated now. Her heart was not encumbered by intense emotions she assumed a girl should have for the man whose baby she carried. Since Tim had left, she was feeling less attachment to him. In his absence she did not feel like he was a part of her life anymore. She did not like to think of herself as a shallow person, but she had to admit her feelings for Tim were less intense since he went away. To be honest, with Tim so far away from her, it was difficult for her to recall their times together. She was beginning to visualize that part of her life more as a dream. It now seemed like a segment of time that had occurred and should be filed away as a memory. Only she could not file away this baby. The baby was no memory. It was alive and growing inside her body.

She was jerked back to present in Janet's bedroom as Janet said, "Frannie, Tim loves you. I know he does. He will be devastated when he finds out you are moving so far away. Don't you want to be Tim's girl anymore?"

Frannie looked at her friend, innocent in her appeal for her brother. Janet did not have any suspicion about Tim's baby growing inside of Frannie. Janet's life was still so uncomplicated. Although Frannie's life was complicated with this unborn child in her, youthful ignorance kept her from consciously accepting her past actions and the impending complications. Her simplicity was evident as she replied to her friend, "Janet, let's be honest with each other. Tim does not truly love me. He likes me a lot. I was his girl while he was still home in Oak Creek. But he's gone now and has so many other things, besides me, to think about. He needs to do well in school. I need to go with my family to California. We are going to have a wonderful life there. Dad and Mom and Reeny will get wonderful jobs and I will go to school there. I may even try acting. We'll be so close to Hollywood. They are starting to make a lot of motion pictures out there. With all the young men coming home from the war' there are many more young people. The newest entertainment craze is movies. After we get settled you can come and visit me there." For the moment Frannie had forgotten about the baby, about her growing body and how big it would be in a few more months. She put her arms around Janet and they snuggled together on the bed as they fell asleep. It was the last time Frannie would spend the night in the Slocum house.

CHAPTER 12

The country was on the move early that year. The war was over. Young men were coming home to their sweethearts and wives. Families were formed. There was a large number of families resulting from the return of America's servicemen. This increase in population necessitated a surge in building new homes across the nation. Returning soldiers were grabbing their women and heading in directions all over the country. After seeing so much destruction in Europe, these men were thankful to return to their country and begin building lives, homes, and families. The McFaddens joined this pulsating vibration of Americans on the move. Stan, after making up his mind to take his family west, quickly decided to put the past behind them all. He did this completely. He sold the home his children were born in. He included the furniture in the sale of the house to avoid having to move it to California. Stella was in complete agreement. Always a stylish woman, she did not want to bring her old fashioned Midwestern furniture into her new modern home in sunny California. Out with the old and in with the new was Stella's way of thinking. Reeny was caught up in the excitement of the changes occurring in all their lives. She still mourned the loss of her young husband and her unborn child, but the intense tragedy of the last few months was lessened by her hope for the future. The plan of her being mother to Frannie's baby aided greatly in healing her damaged heart. It wasn't her own baby, but it was about as close as she could get with Tom being gone. She loved her little sister with her entire heart, and this love would transfer easily to Frannie's baby. This new baby would be hers to raise and love as the child's mother.

Putting their cache of personal belongings into the trunk of the Buick and carrying their dreams for the future in their hearts, the McFadden family climbed into the seats of their Buick and headed for California. They joined a caravan of other dreamers heading toward the sea and sunshine of California. Not since the dust bowl migration of the depression days had Route 66 borne such an exodus of vehicular travel on its winding, rutted two lanes of black pavement. There was an aura of excitement, anticipation, and hope in the air that winter. The country was alive and ready to experience all the happiness promised by peace around the world. The destroying was over and the rebuilding was about to begin. With this same hope in their hearts, the McFaddens traveled miles at a time, each lost in their own thoughts for the future.

Frannie was surprised at the lack of emotion she felt when she thought about Tim. In a way she was ashamed at herself. She had imagined herself in love with him. Now she was leaving his life forever and this realization did not elicit any sadness in her. Feeling this way made it much easier for her to think of her baby as Reeny's baby. In her youth, the spectrum of her emotions was not fully formed. With her lessening feelings for Tim, she felt a lessening of her emotions toward her unborn child. Each day the child within her became more and more her sister's baby. That is how Frannie thought of her baby. It was Reeny's baby. As the two sisters rode in the back seat of the spacious Buick, crossing miles and miles of changing landscape, they talked about their future. In conversation Frannie referred to the baby as Reeny's baby. There was unspoken acceptance that the child now belonged emotionally to Reeny. Frannie accepted her role of birth mother, calm in the knowledge that after she gave birth, her responsibility ended and Reeny's began. Frannie looked over at her sister and said, "Reeny, sometimes I get scared thinking about this baby growing inside me, but then I am happy knowing that I am able to give you this baby to replace your baby. I know it's not the same as your own baby, but we can both love this baby so much. Thank you, Reeny, for taking my baby and for letting me be a part of your life with the baby. I love you, Reeny. You have always been the best sister a girl could have."

Reeny quietly listened to Frannie's childlike acceptance of this solution to her complicated problem. Reeny tried to remember what it felt like to be fifteen years old again. During a relatively short span of time she had lived through a world at war, her first love, marriage, and the death of her husband and unborn child. Undoubtedly, her tragic experiences of this last year made her feel like she had lived far more years than just her biological twenty-one years. So much had happened to her recently she could barely remember what being fifteen years old felt like. Somewhere in her subconscious she could remember the cocoon of safety you lived in as a young teenager. Your mind simply could not accept the complexities of the adult world. Unfortunately, your body surged ahead of your mentality and sometimes thrust you into the paradoxical predicament of a physical situation your mind was too immature to handle. This is what happened to Frannie. Reeny felt far older than her twenty-one years. She decided this might be a good thing, as she prepared herself for the coming challenge of this duplicity she and her family had agreed on. After hours of discussion, the four of them agreed this was the best solution for everyone, and most of all for the innocent child coming into their family. Reeny slid across the backseat and snuggled up to Frannie as they both watched the landscape slide swiftly by them. As she fell asleep, Reeny was thanking the Lord for her parents' help at this very precarious time in her and Frannie's lives.

It was a travel weary group that pulled into Lillian and Herb's driveway in Pasadena just as the warm west coast sunshine was beginning to beckon the afternoon calm. The McFaddens could not contain their enchantment with the warm weather in January. Having lived their entire lives in January's sub-zero, snow laden landscapes of the Midwest, the girls could not contain their joy with the warm weather. They reveled in the sun shining on their skin. They loved not having to bundle up against freezing cold weather. As they stepped out of the Buick, both girls basked in the warm rays of the sun upon their faces. They fell in love with southern California.

"Come on, you doll babies, you must be bushed. You all come into the house now and let's get you all settled," said Aunt Lilian in her singsong, nasal voice. She was Mom's oldest sister and had migrated to California when she was young and just out of nursing school. She worked at a new hospital in Pasadena. Lillian had tried for many years to get Stella to move to California. After being raised in the miserable weather of the Midwest, Lillian thought California was paradise. Now, finally, here was her sister and the whole family together after so many years. She was sure Stan and Stella would love Pasadena. It was a young city but established enough that one could make a solid new beginning here. It was close to everything. Los Angeles was only a forty-five minute drive, and if you went a little farther west you would see the glorious Pacific Ocean. She knew her sister's family had never seen the ocean. It was a thrill to watch someone see the ocean for the first time, and she had planned a special picnic outing for the event. But for now she had to get this migrating family settled into her home until they could get organized and start their new life. The rest of the afternoon they spent unpacking the family's most needed items brought west in the trunk of the Buick. In a way it was sad to leave the accumulation of thirty years of life behind as Stan and Stella had done. On the flip side, they were still young enough to start over. They were in a beautiful new state full of warm sunshine and they were all together. Starting over was the mood permeating the entire country right now. The war was over and life was going to be good. The McFaddens were happy together. In moving to California they seemed to have left the sad things in their life behind them.

After getting settled into their rooms in the big Victorian house where Herb and Lillian had raised their four daughters and two sons, they all gathered for dinner to eat and discuss their immediate plans. Lillian thought she could get Mom and Reeny jobs at the hospital. There were several clerical positions open on different wards, and both were qualified secretaries. Herb was an electrician for a big hotel in downtown Los Angeles, and he was checking to see if the hotel had any accounting positions open that Stan was qualified for.

Although it would be pushing time frames, they decided Frannie should enroll at Pasadena High School, where she could complete her last semester of her junior year. She would attend as long as she could until her pregnancy became too noticeable. Reeny, on the other hand, would work under the pretext of being a pregnant widow. Baggy clothing should suffice long enough to allow Reeny to work for several months. With these plans discussed and everyone in agreement as to their plans for the future, the families went to bed. The McFaddens were tired from their long trip but excited to begin their new lives in this warm and sunny new state that was to be their home now.

CHAPTER 13

Aunt Lillian's kids were all grown and had moved to other cities in California. Aunt Lillian and Uncle Herb never got used to rambling around their big Victorian home by themselves. Having their relatives move in with them brought new life back into the old house. A new daily pattern emerged in their lovely old house. Uncle Herb left early in the morning for his drive into Los Angeles. He was able to get Dad a job in the large hotel's cashiering office. He bragged about Dad being such an asset to the new and growing hotel. It was one of the first high-priced, luxury high-rise hotels built in the rapidly growing city of Los Angeles. He would joke about Dad becoming the CEO of the whole place in no time with his crackerjack accounting skills. Mom and Reeny had both secured jobs at Pasadena Community Hospital where Aunt Lil had worked for the past twenty years. Reeny was a ward clerk on the maternity ward. This job thrilled her. She was able to be around all the newborn babies. Mom was hired as a medical transcriptionist for the hospital doctors. It was perfect for everyone. Mom and Reeny were able to drive the Buick to work and give Aunt Lil a ride with them, as she was working the 7 a.m. to 3 p.m. shift after having paid her dues in the evening and graveyard shifts years ago. Not having to give Lil a ride to the hospital allowed Uncle Herb to adjust his schedule to coincide with Dad's working hours, and they left early together to beat the increasing traffic into downtown Los Angeles. This left Frannie to get herself up each morning and walk the mile to Pasadena High. The awesome sunshine and warm wind made it seem like being in paradise, and she didn't mind the long walk at all. She figured it would keep her in shape as her pregnancy progressed. It soon became apparent to Frannie that everyone in California was blonde, tan, and beautiful. She fit right in with her silver blonde hair and big brown eyes. In no time at all, the boys were attracted to her. Her sweet nature and unsophisticated ways soon attracted the girls to her also. She had lots of friends, made good grades and was adored by her teachers. She was so entrenched in the sunny glow of high school life she could almost forget she was carrying a baby. Sometimes she couldn't believe it was really true. She didn't look much different and she certainly didn't feel different. She was four months pregnant and other than swollen, tender breasts, she didn't notice any other changes in her body. Her stomach was still flat with just the hint of a fleshly layer growing to allow the baby to stretch out as time passed. For the time being she blended in with the other high school kids and forgot about the adult responsibility looming in her future. She left those thoughts to Mom, Dad, and Reeny.

Aunt Lil begged Mom and Dad to stay on in her home. It was a huge Victorian house with room for them all. With three separate floors, it was almost like having apartments. Frannie sensed that Aunt Lil was lonely, left in the big house where all her kids had grown up. She should have moved long ago to a smaller, more modern home. They were popping up all over southern California. Returning serviceman were buying up houses like crazy. These young men were getting married and starting families. Homes were built in record time. Neighborhoods seem to spring up overnight. Where you saw an orange grove one month, you might see a cleared field piled with lumber the next month. Thousands of contractors were ready to start building the homes so desperately needed by the swarm of young, married couples. And babies, it seemed like everywhere you went there were pregnant women, women pushing buggies with newborns in them, women dragging sticky handed toddlers, or carrying young children too tired to walk. It was obvious the young soldiers returning home kept very busy with their wives and sweethearts.

One afternoon Reeny and Frannie were walking in the park under the warm sunshine. It seemed strange to them to walk on green grass beside a bubbling blue creek, with warmth of the sun on their arms, at the end of February. California was indeed the Golden Land. Back home in the Midwest it would be the coldest month of the year, with mountains of snow piled along the roadsides. None of the McFaddens missed the harsh Midwestern winters. As the sisters walked arm in arm, they talked about the coming baby. Reeny had started to wear baggy tops. The baby was due the end of July and Reeny planned to work through May, having people think she was seven months pregnant when she left her job to await the birth of her baby. With all the exercise Frannie was getting, she began to hope she could make it through this semester at school before she began to show her pregnancy. Styles were form fitting and that did not help Frannie's situation. She was lucky, she had a naturally slim form, and so far no one could see any signs of her stomach protruding. With tentative plans laid, each hoping to keep their secret through May, they enjoyed being with each other, planning for what they now called "their" child. At the end of May Frannie could take her finals early if she needed to and complete her junior year of high school. When the month of May ended, Reeny was taking an indefinite leave of absence from the hospital. Mom and Dad decided to stay with Herb and Lil for a few more months. Everyone was happy living together and there was plenty of room in the house. Life settled into a comfortable routine for the rest of that warm California winter.

"Mom, Mom, wake up, Mom, Frannie's crying and moaning and says she's having really bad cramps. I'm afraid, Mom, you better come quick," whispered Reeny, as she shook Stella awake in the wee hours of that warm summer morning at the end of July. Stella, wide awake now, grabbed her wrapper and ran down the hallway to her daughter's bedroom. Immediately she could see Frannie was in heavy labor and scared out of her wits.

"Get Dad, tell him to start the car. The baby is coming," Stella said calmly, as she smiled up at her older daughter. She thought, this baby is just about on time, dear thing. Frannie had been able to keep her pregnancy hidden long enough to finish her junior year of high school. Now they could welcome the new baby as Reeny's child, and life would go on with a new baby to love and pamper. Stella felt calmer now than she had since first learning of the traumatic situation her young daughter had thrust the family into. Finally, the culmination of all their secret plans and unavoidable deceptions was about to take place. Through the tragedies suffered by her older daughter and the lasting mistake made by her younger daughter, finally every effort was coming together to bring her small family some peace and joy. These were the thoughts she had as she held Frannie in her arms, telling her to breathe deeply, trying not to wince as Frannie unmercifully squeezed her hands in her effort to rid herself of the unending pain of childbirth.

Very unconventionally, Mom insisted that she and Reeny be with Frannie when she delivered her baby. Mom knew Reeny needed to see the birth, to bond immediately with the newborn baby. These things needed to happen in this unusual situation where Frannie was the baby's birth mother but Reeny would be the baby's life mother. Mom had argued with the doctors and nurses, bullheadedly insisting on doing it this way. The transfer of this baby from one sister to the other sister must be done exactly right. The well-being of her grandchild and her own daughters depended on a successful transfer of maternal instincts. Mom was doing everything in her power to ensure the success of this emotionally wrenching ordeal. She had counseled both her daughters long and hard about the love that they would each feel for the baby when it was born. She did not want any negative feelings to attach to the love both her girls would feel for this child they had agreed to share. Stalwart, keeping her own emotions in check, she accompanied Reeny and Frannie into the delivery room to watch their baby be born.

With Reeny holding her hand and Mom mopping her sweating brow with a cool rag, Frannie tried to pull herself back to being awake. They had given her some kind of drug to ease the contractions, but she did not like the woosy way it made her head feel. Just as she was able to drift into a dull sleep, the wrenching pains would snap her back to the glaring white light overhead. This ebb and flow feeling in her mind and body was maddening. She wanted this ordeal over with. She had the presence of mind to quickly wonder how any woman could ever go through this agony a second time.

Suddenly, the urge to bear down overtook her and brought her into complete wakefulness. Trying to hold back her screams and holding onto Reeny's hands for dear life, she gave a huge push and within minutes three women welcomed a fourth female into their lives. Healthy, red, and screaming, Laurie Lynn St. Clair entered this world, tying a lifelong knot around these two sisters.

CHAPTER 14

The next two years brought peace and prosperity around the world. It brought new beginnings and happiness to the two families living together in the old Victorian house in Pasadena. It was an odd assortment of age groups living together, but they brought out the best in each other. Four middle-aged adults, two young ladies, and the center of everyone's universe, the precocious, blonde curly headed two-year-old who kept them all young and on their toes. To Reeny, it seemed that once Laurie was born her heart was reborn. From the moment Laurie came into this world and was placed in her waiting arms, Reeny felt complete. The sadness that had been a constant weight in her heart was gone. It had been crowded out by the love that swelled in her for Laurie. The minute she looked into Laurie's unfocused brown eyes, she knew everything would be alright in this world as long as she had this little girl in her life. No sadness could ever again overwhelm her as long as she had Laurie. She never imagined she could love any human being as much as she loved Laurie. Frannie also loved Laurie, but not in the same way. Reeny could not understand Frannie's feelings. Perhaps Frannie had never let herself get too attached to this baby, knowing she could not be the acknowledged mother who would raise her. After Laurie was born, Frannie seemed content to let Mom and Reeny take Laurie from her and tend to all Laurie's immediate needs. Dad decided early on it would be better to let contact with Tim and the Slocums fade out. In time they would forget about Frannie, and he felt the less complications from back home, the better. Reeny thought a great deal about Tom's sister May. She did not feel it was fair to let May suffer any more than she already had with Tom's death. They decided it would be kinder to let May believe this child was Tom's daughter. So they kept in contact with May, letting her believe Reeny was doing fine in California, healthy and ready to deliver a full term baby that summer. Once Laurie was born, snapshots of her were sent off to May and her girls so they could see what she looked like. It was not surprising when May wrote back commenting on how much Laurie took after her Aunt Frannie. They explained away the delayed birth as Reeny having gestational diabetes, which sometimes resulted in longer than normal pregnancies. With May's limited medical knowledge and wanting so much to believe a part of Tom was still on this earth, she did not question any time frames surrounding Laurie's birth. She loved the McFaddens and she loved Laurie. To her they were all part of her family. She had no one except them, now that Tom was gone.

There was no shortage of loving adults to care for Laurie. In those first two years of Laurie's life, Mom, Reeny and Aunt Lil continued to work at the community hospital. They managed to work different shifts so one of them, combined with Frannie's help, was always there to watch Laurie. Frannie finished her senior year, graduated high school and was now finishing her first year of nurse's training at Pasadena Junior College. She loved going to college and felt she had chosen a good career. She helped take care of Laurie, but she could not summon the same maternal concern over Laurie that seemed to come so naturally to Reeny. Sometimes, as she played with Laurie, looking at her, studying her face, she tried to see some resemblance to Tim. The truth was Laurie looked so much like Frannie, it was hard to see any other influence in her features. She had Frannie's soft brown eyes and blonde hair but not as light as Frannie's hair. Laurie's hair had some reddish highlights like Reeny's. It was easy to see Laurie had the McFadden female beauty in her genes. The only thing about Laurie that reminded Frannie of Tim was her wonderfully sweet, shy disposition. She had been the best baby, never cranky or colicky, slept through the night right away, and would let anyone hold her without crying. Mom liked to tell the family that was the kind of baby Reeny had been, passive and sweet natured. As that praise didn't extend over to her babyhood, Frannie rightly assumed she may have been a bit more work that either Laurie or Reeny. The past two years had been a time of healing for them all. Reeny's love for Tom would be forever. He would always have a part of her heart. But she was able to put the hurt behind her and concentrate on raising her little girl. From the moment Laurie was born, Reeny thought of her as the baby she had carried for a few months. In Reeny's mind Laurie was her and Tom's baby girl. She spoke to Laurie often about Tom and this helped her remember all the good things about Tom. She loved bringing Tom back to life in her descriptions of him to Laurie. Laurie was the lifeline this family needed at such a tragic time. As they healed they were able to get on with their lives and take joy in Laurie as she grew from baby to little girl.

Frannie was content to love Laurie as her niece. She could take joy in the baby's antics and not have to deal with the daily complexities of motherhood. She went on with her adolescent growing up that took her through her high school graduation, junior college and eventually advanced nurse's training. During these years she gained the maturity she needed to enter young adulthood.

As the country entered the next decade of the 1950s, it was a much different era than the previous one. Growth was rampant everywhere and in everything. Laurie started school with a huge wave of young children born right after the war ended. When so many young soldiers returned to America after winning the war in Europe, they came home to waiting wives and sweethearts. It was not surprising the years immediately following the war generated an enormous number of babies. This generation of new babies became known as "baby boomers," and would change the world more than any previous generation in history.

No place saw the growth spurt more than California. Los Angeles was gaining renown as the newest metropolitan city forming in postwar America. Highways were being built with unstoppable speed. The city became like an octopus, with all roads leading to a vibrating hub teaming with young entrepreneurs anxious to build their city while making their own pots of gold. Pasadena was like an older, maidenly aunt to the new city of angels. People lived and raised children in Pasadena while husbands commuted to Los Angles to earn the paychecks keeping their wives and children in stylish suburban lifestyles.

Part of Frannie's advanced nurse's training took her into downtown Los Angeles to study at the medical center located within the University of Los Angeles. Frannie loved studying at UCLA. It was like a small medical city within the great big city of Los Angeles. Within the two mile radius of the medical center and the university there existed a close knit city of medical professionals all living and breathing their desire to cure the ailments causing human suffering. Research was priority and Frannie loved being involved in new discoveries in medicine. There was a surge in the study of mental illness, with emphasis on drug therapy as well as electroshock therapy. Frannie's interest was piqued by the psychological nursing classes she was introduced to at UCLA. She felt she was being given a cursory view of a field of study so complex and enormous, it would consume the best minds in the country for many future decades. In the years to come she would remember her sharp interest in a heretofore unexplored area of medicine, that of the human brain, chemical interaction and the combination of both on human emotions. As these variables began to affect her own life, she would reflect on her early premonition that studying mental illness and human emotions would be pushed to the forefront of interest in the very near future. She had a premonition that repercussions would eventually result from mounting human emotions based on the lifestyle of a nation crazed with immediate gratification.

CHAPTER 15

Frannie had been riding the bus system from Pasadena to UCLA for several months and was noticing the attractive, slender young man who rode in with her each day but must have returned on a different bus. For the past five years Frannie did not pay much attention to men. She was content to be with her extended family. She reveled in her learning and loved her field of study, psychiatric nursing. She took great joy in her role as Laurie's loving aunt and she was very content with her life. But now, she realized she was attracted to the gentleman who rode her bus each day. Perhaps she was admitting she was young and lonely. She was twenty-one years old, and other than giving birth to Laurie had not really experienced much of life. As she traveled into Los Angeles day after day, she began to suspect she would not be content to remain in her family's home in Pasadena. Much as she loved them, she began to admit she needed a life of her own. She remained in casual contact with Janet Slocum after she moved to California. Janet had graduated high school and married right after graduation. The last Christmas card she received updated her on the birth of Janet's second son. In the correspondence, Frannie learned that Tim had graduated with honors and was engaged to a girl he met at Northwestern. They were both twenty-three years old with successful careers in their futures. Frannie was happy for Tim. She begrudged him nothing, wanting only his happiness. As she grew up and Laurie grew older, she sometimes experienced a pang of guilt in withholding the knowledge from Tim that he had a daughter. But Laurie's life was set in its pattern now and Frannie would do nothing to alter or upset the even keel of Laurie's life. She assuaged her guilt feelings by reassuring herself that Tim would have a successful life with other children to love and cherish.

As Frannie was getting to know her fellow bus rider, Reeny also was becoming romantically interested in a doctor she was introduced to at the hospital where she had worked for the past five years. As Laurie started kindergarten, Reeny began dating her handsome, young doctor friend, Brad Lawrence. By the time Laurie's school had open house for parents, Brad was smitten with both Reeny and Laurie and was proud to be included in the family's visit to Laurie's kindergarten class. Laurie seemed unaware that her family was different than the other kids' families. She had a large extended family. Mom, Aunt Frannie, Grandma, Grandpa, Aunt Lillian, Uncle Herb, and now Brad Lawrence, all lined up to meet Laurie's teacher and review her academic progress. Laurie loved all these adults in her life and never seemed to realize she was different with no siblings. She had friends with siblings, but she was still too young to wonder why she was an only child. Reeny thought of this aspect of Laurie's life often and was especially glad to have Brad in her life. She had dreams of a future with Brad and having children, giving Laurie brothers and sisters.

One evening Frannie and Reeny were sitting in the big living room by themselves catching up on each other's lives. As Frannie listened to Reeny talk about Brad, she could see Reeny's love for him in her eyes. A strange feeling of alarm quickly passed through Frannie's chest. She began to realize there was a serious relationship between Brad and Reeny. Perhaps she had not realized it before, because she thought Reeny would always love Tom, and never acknowledged that perhaps Reeny also wanted a more complete life, one with a husband and more children. This thought scared Frannie. A change in Reeny's life might separate her from Laurie. Deep down inside Frannie knew this was always a possibility. She had suppressed this reality and kept it buried. But now it was digging its way out, and she instinctively knew she would have to face this possibility in the near future. She could see her sister was falling in love and repercussions from changes in Reeny's life would affect her also.

"You're very serious about Brad, aren't you, Reeny," said Frannie, as the two of them sat in the living room.

"Yes, Frannie, I am. Brad has asked me to marry him. I want to marry him, Frannie. I've known I must talk with you about this, but I did not know where to begin. I love you so much, Frannie. I would never do anything to hurt you. If I marry Brad it means taking Laurie away from this house where we have all lived together since she was born. It means taking her away from you, not totally of course, but it will not be the same as us living together like we are doing now. Oh, Frannie, this has all been tearing at my heart. I love Brad and Laurie, and I want Laurie to have a daddy and brothers and sisters, but it kills me to know that she won't be with you each day. Please, Frannie, tell me how you feel," pleaded Reeny with tears in her eyes.

Strangely enough, Frannie felt she was the calmer of the two women. She felt as if she were the older of the two. Very calmly she took Reeny's hands into her own and said, "Reeny, you are Laurie's mother. You are my sister and my best friend. You saved me from a very complex situation when you became Laurie's mother. I owe you my life and my happiness. I love Laurie with all my heart, but to me, you are Laurie's mother. I want you to be happy and I want Laurie to be happy. That is what will make me happy. You deserve a real family, a husband, and more children. You buried Tom in the ground more than five years ago. You do not have to bury him in your heart, but you do have to move on, for your sake and for Laurie's. Put Tom in the past where he belongs and go forward with your new love. Make a new life for yourself and your daughter. I will always be here for you and for Laurie. We are family, the three of us. Nothing can ever change that. But we are both young. It is time to move forward and find love. We both deserve that, Reeny. The world is alive with happiness. Big, noisy families are everywhere. I want that for you and me and Laurie. So, Reeny, you tell Brad you'll marry him. Make it a quick engagement. You don't want Laurie to be much older than her brothers and sisters, do you?" laughed Frannie, as she hugged Reeny close to her.

Reeny and Brad were married in a beautiful Christmas ceremony with Laurie looking like an angel as she walked down the aisle tossing red rose petals on the ground. Only in warm, sunny southern

California would you find roses still blooming in December. The day of the wedding was sunny and warm with blue skies and green grass. As Stan walked his beautiful daughter down the aisle, he reflected on the winter beauty of California and thought how very different the icy cold winters of Midwest were. Hard to believe it was the same planet. He was happy and content, glad he had brought his family out west over five years ago. Things had worked out well for them all, and now his girls had a chance at true happiness. Here was Reeny, marrying a great guy who would be a wonderful father for Laurie. Frannie's new beau sat in the front pew with Stella. Stan had a feeling it wouldn't be much longer when he would be walking Frannie down this very same church aisle. God, he wanted his girls to be happy. As he delivered Reeny to her new husband-to-be, he said a short prayer of thanks and sat down beside Stella.

Frannie stood beside her beautiful sister when Reeny was married for the second time. No one was forgetting Tom, they were just moving on with life. May and her two daughters had traveled out west for Reeny's wedding. This gesture had meant so much to Reeny. She had been afraid May would resent her marrying Brad. But May was like Tom, so good-hearted and wanting the best for Reeny. Brad and May hit it off perfectly. You could not help but love May. She was good and kind to everyone. Although May's daughters were several years older than Laurie, they were her only cousins, and they were girls so that made it perfect. The three of them were glued together, whispering, giggling, and sleeping all three in one double bed. Laurie loved being part of a family with other kids in it. May and her girls, along with Laurie, were all staying in Aunt Lil's big house until Brad and Reeny returned from their honeymoon.

One evening after the girls were asleep, May and Frannie sat in the kitchen talking. May said, "Frannie, I am so happy Reeny found Brad. I worried about her after Tom died. It's not right that Reeny should mourn Tom forever. Don't think bad of me, Frannie, but I regret not looking around after my husband died. I should have found me another husband, given my girls a stepfather. But I was too hurt, too unsure of myself. Now it's too late. I'm not young anymore and the girls are almost grown, but I'm lonely and have been for years. I'm glad that won't be the case with Reeny and Laurie. I loved my brother Tom, and he was a good man, but he's dead, and Reeny and Laurie can move on now and give their love to Brad. Tom will always be a part of their lives, but he needs to be in his place in their past and Brad is their future. And you, Frannie, you need to marry that handsome young lawyer you brought to the wedding. His name was Philip, wasn't it? Yes, that was it, Philip Sommers. I remember thinking what a distinguished name that was for a lawyer. I can see the fireworks going on between you two. I know he looks all too studious and is so quiet, but you mark my words, 'still waters run deep.'"

Frannie burst out laughing as she said, "Oh, May, you are dramatic tonight. I love you so much. Yes, you're right. I love Philip and we plan on getting married. I didn't want to overshadow Reeny's big day, but next summer is my turn. We want to have a family very soon after we get married. With any luck, it won't be too long before Laurie has brothers, sisters, and more cousins. I wish you and the girls lived out here in California. Have you ever considered moving here, May? You're family and you should be out here with us. The girls need to get to know Laurie and grow up around her."

May was quiet and serious looking as she replied, "Yes, Frannie, I have thought about moving. The Midwest winters are getting hard on me. I have arthritis and my joints bother me a lot in the cold weather. But I'm a working woman and I need to consider money. I've been thinking I could sell Mom and Dad's house. They left it to me and Tom, and then when Tom died it was all mine. The money would give me a nest egg to get me by until I found a job here. I'm a good secretary, and Los Angeles is booming, and secretaries make a good salary out here. I've been checking around while I've been here. I was thinking I could talk to Philip about legal secretary jobs and see what's available in Los Angeles. I think it's almost time me and the girls got out of that snow." She gave Frannie a big smile and a hug as she got up to go to bed.

Two weeks later, as May and the girls boarded the Santa Fe Chief for the three day train ride back, they kissed everyone goodbye. They left with promises to begin packing and making plans to sell the house. Hopefully May and her daughters would be heading back to California when the school year finished. They wanted to be back in Pasadena in time for Frannie and Philip's summer wedding. Laurie and her cousins vowed they would never be separated again after they were reunited next summer.

CHAPTER 16

After seeing May off at the railway station, Philip and Frannie decided to stay in Los Angeles. Tomorrow they would travel north to the rapidly growing city of Hollywood. Philip was meeting with representatives from one of the new movie studios. Hollywood was cranking out new movies faster than they could find new actors and actresses. The city was swelling with beautiful, hopeful movie stars. And all these movie moguls, actors, and starlets needed legal beagles to keep the fine print on the contracts from exploding in the courtrooms. Without telling anyone their exact plans, they had booked a room at the Knickerbocker Hotel in Hollywood. Tonight would be their first night together. They had talked about waiting until the wedding night, but decided to experience each other now. They were both ready. They wanted each other and felt they were mature enough to handle their emotional and physical relationship now. Their wedding date was set for the coming summer, but they were hungry for each other now. Philip, with his exacting and analytical nature, had outlined all these considerations. Frannie, with her youthful exuberance, simply wanted to love Philip and explore the sexual intimacies she had briefly experienced with Tim when she was too young to fully appreciate the joys two people could find in each other's bodies. She was ready, willing, and excited about spending the night with Philip tonight. Unlike her first sexual experience, she was prepared this time. She was well acquainted with her body, her desires, and her contraceptives. No accidental pregnancies. Her life was well-planned. She had been fortunate last time. Her youthful mistake and resulting pregnancy had not been the disaster it could have been, thanks to her family's love and support. Laurie was the most wonderful child, and she brought great joy to everyone in her life. Frannie was older now and wanted her children planned and welcomed into a family with both a mother and a father.

They arrived late in the afternoon and checked into their room as Mr. and Mrs. Philip Sommers. Frannie felt mysterious and clandestine. She became excited when she thought about what would happen soon between her and Philip. They had planned to unpack and go to dinner, but the minute they were in their bedroom, they both knew they wouldn't be able to wait to experience their joy in each other. After setting down their suitcases, they looked at each other, smiled, and wrapped their arms around each other. The air between them sparked with passion as they began kissing and letting their hands explore each other's body. As Frannie stretched up to meet Philip's full lips, she felt warmth developing between her legs. As their lips clung together, they stumbled over to the bed. After several moments of kissing and fondling each other, they took off their clothing. As they lie down on top of the bed, seeing each other naked for the first time, they smiled, pleased with each other's anatomy. The next kiss was all it took to get them both excited. As Philip lifted his legs over Frannie's softly arched body and entered her, his penis quickly finding her smooth, slick vagina, she cried out in pleasure as she guided him by holding his buttocks, urging him to go faster and harder as she approached a quick orgasm in the newness of the experience, combined with her youthful body's ability to react quickly to Philip's sexual stimulations. It was over much too soon, but both had experienced their first orgasm together. They rolled over onto their backs, happy in their coupling. They were satisfied with each other's bodies. Each was pleased with the other's abilities in their newly entered sexual arena. Holding each other in their nakedness, they fell asleep, happy in their expectations of an active and pleasurable marriage.

Frannie was content, feeling that she had finally put the past in its place. She recognized her immature passion for Tim as an adolescent passage that had resulted in Laurie's birth. Now with Laurie growing up as Reeny's daughter, Frannie felt safe putting that phase of her life behind her. She looked forward to her role as Philip's wife and mother of his children. She felt no guilt in not revealing Laurie's true identity to Philip. She felt strongly that part of her life belonged in her past. She felt it was best for her family to keep the secret of Laurie's birth between herself, Reeny, Mom and Dad. She had lived the lie of being Laurie's aunt for so long. She had no wish to complicate her life at this time when everything was going so well for everyone. Reeny had just married a wonderful man who would be a perfect father for Laurie, and she was soon to marry Philip. Everything was going smoothly, so let sleeping dogs lie.

Philip was pleased with his business trip to Hollywood and announced to Frannie that he was accepting a position with a prestigious theater arts law firm. This meant he and Frannie would relocate to Hollywood. He was concerned about the effect this move would have on Frannie and her family. He knew how close she was to her sister and her niece. Frannie assured him that Hollywood was not so far from Pasadena as to be a problem. She knew she could get a nursing job anywhere, and Philip should take his job offer in Hollywood. He had a great career opportunity ahead of him. Frannie planned to quit working as soon as she started having her children, so it was important for Philip to further his career. With the move settled on, they went forward with plans for their summer wedding.

During the next few months, as Reeny and Brad got settled in their own home in Pasadena, the family's attention shifted to Frannie's wedding. Occasionally the reality of being away from her close-knit family would cause Frannie to stop and dwell on the strangeness of being out of the immediate circle she was so accustomed to. With Reeny and Laurie already moved out of Aunt Lil's house, she was beginning to accept being separated from them. Life was propelling her ahead at a rapid pace. So many changes were taking place in her life. She never allowed herself to think of Laurie as her own daughter. Beginning from Laurie's birth, she sorted out her emotions and accepted her role as Laurie's aunt. Now, after more than five years as an aunt instead of a mother, she could cope with the fact she would not see Laurie everyday. It was harder to deal with Reeny not being in her life everyday. For over twenty-one years they had never been apart for more than a few days at a time. The demands of youth were pressing and both sisters had chosen their separate pathways. The emotions evoked by their separation were powerful, but each woman was comforted by the new love in her life and the joys they had shared in the past. With strong hearts filled with hope for the future, they each went on with their own lives. Frannie and Reeny knew that no matter where the winds of time blew them, they would always be connected through their love for each other and the secret they shared in Laurie.

CHAPTER 17

Frannie and Philip had been living in Hollywood for over a year when Frannie got a frantic call from Laurie. Her squeaky voice came over the telephone. "Aunt Frannie, Mommy won't get out of bed. There is no food in our house, and Daddy has been away for a week. Mommy told me not to call Grandma and Grandpa, but I'm hungry and she won't wake up. Please come and get me, Aunt Frannie."

Frannie tried to calm Laurie down as she said, "Stay with your mother, Laurie. I'm leaving now and will be at your house in about two hours. You can watch your new television set. Aren't they great, so much fun to watch. You can turn it on. That will keep you company until I can get there."

After hanging up the telephone, Frannie maneuvered her large stomach up the stairs to get her hat and coat. She was going into her sixth month of pregnancy and climbing the stairs was a chore. She called Philip at the studio office and left a message that she was going to Pasadena for the day. She was worried about Laurie and Reeny. She was so busy with her new home in Hollywood. She had become pregnant so soon after her wedding, she had lost track of time and hadn't kept in touch with Reeny as often as she should have. She was so happy in her new life as the pregnant wife of a successful movie star lawyer, she had been remiss in her old role as sister and auntie. She had also given up her dreams of pursuing her own career in psychiatric nursing. Just a year ago that field of nursing had consumed her interest. It was new and the things being learned were amazing. Studies being done at this time in the early 1950s were enlightening. The dark ages of mental illness were being shown new light. Frannie had just gotten her interest piqued when she put it all on hold to become Philip's wife. Now with this baby coming, she wondered if she would ever get back to working in that field again. Right now she had to get to Pasadena. Something was very wrong with Reeny. She had been so remiss in contacting Reeny and Laurie. Her guilt was threatening to overwhelm her. Tucking her big belly behind the steering wheel, she eased the clutch out on the '51 Thunderbird she had received as a wedding present from Philip. When she first saw it she was delighted with the shiny red color and sporty white convertible top. Now her stomach barely fit behind the wheel. She felt ridiculous and knew her car would soon be traded in for a sleek new Oldsmobile station wagon. Driving her sporty convertible, she put the top down. She was determined to enjoy the impracticality of the car for as long as she could. She enjoyed the warm California sunshine and orange scented breeze blowing through her long, silvery blonde hair as she drove east towards Pasadena.

Frannie set the parking brake on the T-bird, wedged herself out of the car, and headed in the front door of Reeny and Brad's sprawling ranch home nestled in the cool foothills of east Pasadena. She immediately noticed the gloom within the lovely home. All the draperies were pulled shut against the lazy noon sunshine. The house smelled closed up and musty. She called out for Laurie, who came running into the dining room to meet Frannie.

As Laurie threw herself into Frannie's arms and laid her head against Frannie's bulging stomach, she cried, "Aunt Frannie, it's so awful here now. Daddy is gone all the time working at the hospital and Mommy is always sad. She cries a lot and sleeps all the time. No one takes care of me and I am hungry."

A quick look around the room confirmed Laurie's report. Dust was an inch thick on the massive oak dining table and buffet. Taking Laurie into the kitchen with her, she opened some canned Campbell's soup and quickly heated it up on the stove. She set a bowl and spoon on the small kitchen table and left Laurie eating soup and crackers as she went in search of Reeny.

"What has gotten into you, Reeny?" said Frannie, as she tried to wake her sister up. She shook Reeny hard but still Reeny slept. Frannie's attention was drawn to the prescription bottle on the night stand. Picking it up, she saw it was a prescription for sleeping pills.

Alarmed, she began to shake Reeny. This seemed to have some effect on Reeny, as she moaned and tried to sit up in bed. "What is wrong with you, Reeny?" demanded Frannie. In a loud voice she commanded, "Wake up! Laurie called me. She is hungry. You can't sleep all day and leave her to take care of herself. She's just a little girl. Good God, Reeny, it's past noon. Why are you still sleeping? What are you doing taking sleeping pills? Reeny, wake up and tell me what the hell is going on here."

Slowly Reeny's dull eyes focused on Frannie. After taking a sip of water from her bedside glass, Reeny said, "Frannie, I'm so sorry, I didn't know what time it was. I couldn't sleep last night. I can't sleep at night anymore. The doctor gave me some pills to help me go to sleep at night. Without them, I'm up wandering all night long. I flop from bed to bed and still I can't sleep. It bothers Brad and keeps him awake, so he started sleeping at the hospital."

Reeny glanced at Frannie's big stomach and her eyes filled with tears as she said, "Frannie, why aren't I pregnant yet? Brad and I keep trying and nothing has happened. We have been trying for two years and still I don't get pregnant. He doesn't understand it. He doesn't say anything, but I know he wonders why it is taking so long. He believes Laurie is my daughter, and he figures I got pregnant with her right after I married Tom. He's beginning to wonder if there is something wrong with him. Oh, Frannie, what if the miscarriage damaged something in me and that's why I haven't gotten pregnant. I can't talk to Brad about it. He thinks I gave birth to Laurie. He doesn't know anything about the baby I lost."

Reeny reached over and clutched Frannie's arms in her hands as she said, "Frannie, I'm scared. Maybe we were wrong in not telling our husbands the truth about Laurie. Maybe we should have been honest and let Laurie know you are really her mother. I will always love Laurie as if she were my natural daughter. No one could love Laurie the way I do. To me, she is my natural daughter. I feel like I gave birth to her. I was there when she came out of your body and it felt like she was coming out of mine. I felt that close to her when she was born. But, Frannie, let's be honest. Other people won't understand about you and me and Laurie and why we lied about who was Laurie's mother. I'm afraid that Brad won't understand, that he'll feel I deceived him. Frannie, I have always felt like Laurie really was my baby. I didn't want anything to change the way it was for the five years of her life before I met Brad. I wish I would get pregnant then everything would be perfect."

Frannie remained calm in the face of Reeny's anguish. She took Reeny's hands and said, "No, Reeny, you can't tell anyone about Laurie. We have lived with our secret for too long now to change it. Laurie is the one we have to think of. She is your daughter, only yours. She is my niece. That is how I have always felt. I do not have the maternal love for her that you have. Yes, I love her with all my heart, but I have always been second to you in her life. She needs you, Reeny. She needs you to be the mother you have always been to her. You took her when I could not be her mother and you became her mother. Please, Reeny, don't stop now. The job is not done. It will never be done. You are her mother and you will always be her mother."

It was as if the two sisters had changed places, and for the first time Frannie became the more mature sister as she tried to reason with Reeny. Frannie continued in her soft, soothing voice saying, "Reeny, I am going to become a mother myself soon, and for the first time I feel like I am ready for that job. I cannot be Laurie's mother. It is too late for those kinds of feelings. They must come from you. I am her aunt. That is all I can be. If you were not here for her then I would take her and love her and mother her in your place. However, I can never be the mother that you are to her. Get hold of yourself, Reeny. You must pull yourself out of this depression. Brad and Laurie need you."

The two sisters hugged and held each other as Reeny promised Frannie she would concentrate on getting well. Frannie stayed with Reeny and Laurie the rest of the day and was relieved when Brad showed up for dinner. She could tell from the concerned look in his eyes as he fussed over Laurie that he was worried about his family. Later that night, when Reeny went to put Laurie to bed, Brad cornered Frannie in the kitchen and asked what brought her to Pasadena. Frannie explained Laurie's call to Brad and expressed her concern about Reeny. Shaking his head, Brad said, "Yes, Frannie, I am getting worried about her. She is depressed for days on end. She doesn't sleep at night. She wants to get pregnant so badly. I think she places too much importance on having another child. God knows, I would like another child too, but if it's not to be, I can live with that. I love Laurie and I feel blessed to have her as my daughter. Getting Reeny was the cake and having Laurie as my daughter is the icing on that cake. I can live with that, Frannie. Having Reeny as my wife and Laurie as my daughter is enough for me. Why can't that be enough for Reeny?" Brad looked so sad and confused.

"We'll just have to stand by her and get her through these hard days. Surely this depression she's in can't last forever. You're a doctor, Brad. Aren't there new drugs to treat depression these days?" asked Frannie.

Brad answered her seriously, saying, "Yes, Frannie, there is a lot of research being done in the field of depression, schizophrenia, and electroshock therapy. But I want to go conservatively with Reeny's problems right now. I'm hoping with support from her family she will come to realize that we can be happy as a family, just she and I and Laurie. We are a family, just the three of us. She has to see that. I want her to be happy. If another baby will make her happy then I hope it happens. But if she doesn't get pregnant again, I want her to love Laurie and me. I want her to accept that. I want the two of us to be enough for her. Why can't we be enough for her?" Brad's sad and confused look nearly brought tears to Frannie's eyes as she tried to comfort him.

Reeny's depression deepened as months went by without her conceiving. She kept hoping and praying but to no avail. She was afraid to see a fertility specialist, thinking that somehow the secret of her miscarriage would come out. She began to develop paranoia that Brad would discover the truth about Laurie. For the few remaining months before Frannie gave birth, Reeny managed to pull herself together enough to care for Laurie and Brad. Her family was hopeful their old Reeny was returning. For a while, Reeny quit dwelling on her inability to conceive and doted on Laurie, making Brad think the worst was over. He began to hope that Reeny was accepting him and Laurie as her complete family now.

CHAPTER 18

Early in March, 1952, Frannie gave birth to a son. He was christened Stephen Thomas Sommers. Stan and Stella were thrilled with their first grandson, but no child would ever be as close to them as Laurie was. Only they knew the secret of Laurie's birth, other than their daughters. But here was this little boy. He was born under such different circumstances. He was a sweet darling for them to shower with love and affection. Finally, Frannie had a child she could claim as her own. She was old enough and she was married. She vowed to be the best mother Stephen could ever hope for. She reveled in caring for Stephen. With her maturity came the maternal instincts she had lacked when Laurie was born. Together, she and Stephen bonded in a way Frannie had never experienced before. She felt that as long as Stephen was in her world, all as was right with the universe. The only other person who made her feel the world was perfect with them in it was Reeny. She loved Laurie, but she had never felt this fierce protectiveness towards her as she did for Stephen. Perhaps it was because she had been so young when Laurie was born. She had not been mature enough to protect anyone. Reeny had been there to step in as Laurie's mother. Laurie had not needed Frannie's protection as Stephen did now. Frannie dismissed any guilt over loving Stephen more than Laurie and went on with her newfound joy in motherhood.

During the first year of Stephen's life, May and her girls finally moved out to Hollywood. May had planned to move west after Reeny and Brad married, but she waited until her girls finished high school. Now they were both in college, and May brought them to California, as she heard the colleges in California were affordable and anxious to accept female students. Philip got May a job at his law firm in Hollywood, and May and her girls rented a nice apartment bungalow in West Hollywood. May and her two girls were thrilled to be part of Reeny and Frannie's families. They had been so alone in the

Midwest. May told Reeny the only thing she regretted leaving was Tom's grave. She felt badly that no family lived there to go and put flowers on Tom's gravesite. She comforted herself knowing Tom would not want her to stay just for that reason. He was too good a man to begrudge anyone happiness.

Laurie was thrilled with her grownup girl cousins. She felt like she had the greatest family in the world. She had her glamorous college student cousins and also her baby cousin, Stephen. She doted on Stephen like a big sister. She had relatives in Hollywood and in Pasadena. She loved Brad and thought he was the best daddy a girl could ask for. Her grandma and grandpa and Aunt Lil and Uncle Herb lived in a huge Victorian house where she loved to spend the night. Sometimes Aunt Frannie and Uncle Philip left Stephen there with her so Grandma and Grandpa would babysit them both. That was the best time, when she and Stephen stayed at Aunt Lil's with all of the older folks, as Mommy called them. It made Laurie sad when she thought about her mommy. Her mommy was always sad. Whenever Stephen was around, Mommy would hold him and talk to him, and Laurie felt like Mommy liked Stephen more than she liked her. So Laurie would act up to get her mother's attention. This got her into trouble and Reeny would become even more depressed after having to scold Laurie. It was frustrating for Laurie. She was confused and didn't know why her mother didn't love her as much since Stephen was born. Laurie wished her mommy would have a baby too. She wanted a brother or sister. Whenever she asked her mommy about having a baby, her mommy would cry so Laurie quit asking her about it.

When Stephen was two years old, Frannie gave birth to a baby girl. She was named Emily. Everyone doted on this beautiful new baby. Her father was successful in the entertainment industry representing famous stars in Hollywood. She had inherited her father's big dark eyes and European looks. She promised to be a great beauty in the years to come. Frannie was kept busy with her growing family, content and happy with her life. She spent many afternoons basking in the glow of happiness brought to her by mothering her two young children. That pleasure, coupled with being the wife of a successful entertainment attorney, made Frannie think her life was just about perfect.

The sudden intrusion of the doorbell brought Frannie's attention back to the present. After making sure Emily was tucked warmly beneath her baby blanket in her crib, Frannie went downstairs. Opening the elegant oak door, she was surprised to see Brad and Laurie on her front porch. After ushering them into the foyer, she looked at Laurie's confused face and quickly surmised she better speak with Brad alone. After sending Laurie upstairs to play with Stephen, she directed Brad into the kitchen. Sitting down with cups of hot tea, she waited for Brad's explanation.

"I'm sorry to have to sound so heartless, Frannie," apologized Brad, "but I think it's the best thing I can do for her. She's depressed far past the point of being able to handle it on her own. Reeny needs more help than I can give her. For her sake and for Laurie's safety, I had to make this decision." Brad had come to ask Frannie if she could watch Laurie.

Reeny's depression had gotten worse over the last two years, and Brad had finally committed her to a sanatorium in San Diego. He was hopeful the warm sea breezes and lack of stress and responsibility would soon restore his wife to the girl she was when he had married her. That seemed so long ago. They had been so happy when they first got married. Reeny loved being his wife. Then, as a few years went by and no babies came along, Reeny began to fall into this depression she could not pull herself out of. For years Brad hoped she would accept that Laurie was the only child she would have. He kept hoping that would be enough for her. But it seemed as if Reeny became more depressed as time went on. Each time Frannie became pregnant, Reeny tried to hide the sorrow of her own inability to conceive. Brad could tell Frannie's pregnancies just compounded Reeny's feelings of failure. Finally, he became so worried over Reeny's lack of interest in her world and in taking care of Laurie, he feared for Laurie's safety. Also, he could see a change coming over Laurie. She was not the happy, laughing little girl he had been given as a daughter. She was growing up and she should be having fun. He couldn't stand to see Laurie withdrawing into herself. She was afraid to bring her friends home because she never knew what shape she would find her mother in. Laurie was barely ten years old, and he could see she was taking care of her mother more than Reeny was taking care of her. He had been remiss in his duty as her father. He had buried his head in the sand for too long now. Much as he hoped things would change by themselves, he had finally accepted Reeny was not able to help herself. He had finally faced up to his responsibility as husband and father. After much crying and arguing, he had convinced Reeny to go into the sanatorium for therapy, begging her to think of Laurie. She was missing out on Laurie's childhood. In a few more years Laurie would be a teenager, and Reeny spent most of her days in bed, drugged with sleeping pills. She was not setting a good example for Laurie and she needed help. With Brad's coaxing she agreed to go to San Diego for six month's rest and therapy in a fancy new 'respite' care sanatorium.

Frannie fixed up a bedroom for Laurie. For the first time since she gave birth to Laurie, she was caring for her on a daily basis. Frannie was not used to seeing Laurie in this sullen, withdrawn state. Laurie had always been so happy. Now she was quiet, sad, and rarely laughed or talked. Overnight she had lost the daily presence of her mother and father in her life. She loved her Aunt Frannie and Uncle Philip, but it was not the same as living with her mother and father. Brad tried hard to maintain a reliable presence in his daughter's life. He came on the weekends to visit Laurie or to take her on special weekend outings, trying to make up for the drastic change in her life. To Frannie, Laurie seemed like the saddest little girl alive. Frannie was frantic to know what to do to help her. To the world, Laurie was her niece, but Frannie knew this was her little daughter who was suffering so much. The ache of being unable to make Laurie happy twisted painfully in Frannie's heart.

As the months went by, Laurie became immersed in the daily routine of her Aunt Frannie's household. Slowly but surely, as all children do, she adapted. By summer vacation she was feeling loved by and a part of Frannie's young family. She loved the baby, Emily, and doted on her toddler cousin, Stephen. Frannie was growing very close to Laurie and this worried her. She did not want to usurp Reeny's place as Laurie's mother. She had always been content to be Laurie's aunt. Laurie seemed to need her so much right now. It was only natural for her to respond to this need. As Reeny stayed in the sanatorium trying to understand the awful depression that enveloped her, Frannie and Laurie experienced a bonding new to both of them. As time passed Frannie quit feeling guilty about mothering Laurie, and they both reveled in their newfound joy in each other.

Brad came to visit Laurie and saw how happy and content she had become living with Frannie and Philip. Sometimes he became sad as he watched the joy Laurie experienced being part of Frannie's family. It was a joy that had so eluded him and Reeny and Laurie. He quit torturing himself with endless wondering why Reeny could not be content with him and Laurie. He continued his visits to see Laurie, but she seemed more a part of Frannie's family. He felt it best at this time to let Laurie blend in with this whole and healthy family.

One evening after the kids were all in bed, Brad said the Frannie, "Reeny seems to be getting much better. They have been doing electroshock therapy on her. At first I hated to let her go through that, but I can see it calms her down. Frannie, she gets so agitated. She talks about weird things. When she is very agitated she tells me God is punishing her for deceptions she has committed. She raves on and on about her first husband, Tom. She talks to herself, saying over and over the truth will set her free. I don't know what she is talking about. I don't even care about what went on in her life before I met her. She has a right to her past. I would never question anything she did before I met her. I accepted her just as she was when I met her. That is the Reeny I loved then and still love now. I have always said Laurie was an added bonus. She is haunted by past demons that she needs to let go of if she is ever going to get well."

After listening to Brad, Frannie was so tempted to tell him the truth about Laurie. But she knew she could not do that. Too many lives would be affected. No, the truth had been kept a secret for so long, and it must go on that way. Reeny would have to fight her demons and pull herself out of this depression, or she was in grave danger of losing the daughter she had loved from birth.

CHAPTER 19

For the next five years Reeny fought the battle of mental illness with Brad always at her side. Through simple default, Frannie became Laurie's mother. Reeny was not able to continue raising Laurie. Her mind was too fragile. Brad continued to play as much a role in Laurie's life as time would permit. He was kept busy at the hospital in Pasadena and visiting Reeny in San Diego. It was easier during these five years to let Laurie blend in with Philip and Frannie and their two children. Brad would come and get Laurie and take her to San Diego to visit her mother. Laurie loved her mother, but was too young to understand mental illness. She could not comprehend why her mother did not get well and come home so they could be a family together again. Her youth did not permit her to ponder the enormity of this question for very long. Reeny was being treated with the newest methods of controlling manic-depressive behavior. She was given electroshock therapy. Benefits from this therapy were not yet well documented, but the immediate benefit was a calming effect on the patient. To Laurie, her mom seemed strange, quiet, and withdrawn. Her mother was not the same happy mom Laurie remembered from early childhood. She felt uncomfortable around her mother at the hospital. She did not want to have to adapt to Reeny's illness by being quiet and well-behaved all the time. Instead, she simply accepted her fate of living with her Aunt Frannie, and left her father to deal with her mother's illness. She loved her Aunt Frannie deeply and it was easy to fit into Frannie's young and growing family. She soon lost her feelings of loneliness at not having her own mother in her life. Once again, she became the bubbly, blonde child she was meant to be. Often times as Frannie watched Laurie playing outside with the sun shining on her pale silver hair, she realized how lucky she was to have Laurie in her life. Too young when Laurie was born to own up to motherhood, she had been blessed with the opportunity of being Laurie's aunt. Trying hard to remain loyal to Reeny and the bargain they had struck so many years ago, Frannie held fast to her position of being auntie to Laurie. She made a point of talking about Reeny to Laurie so she would not forget what a wonderful mother she had. Deep inside she knew she reveled in this time of having Laurie all to herself, secretly loving her as only a mother could love her daughter. But she never put aside the thought that someday Laurie would return to Reeny and Brad. As the days turned in months, which turned into years, Frannie came to accept that her love for Laurie would never again be the same as it was before Laurie came to live with her.

Laurie's fifteenth birthday ushered in the 1960s. Laurie's life had taken on a routine of living between several homes. She lived with her mom and Brad whenever Reeny was "normal." This meant Reeny was well enough or sedated enough to leave the sanatorium that had become her second home. If Reeny was having a "bad spell," she went to live with Frannie and Philip. Once she started high school, she began to stay with her grandma and grandpa whenever Reeny went back to the sanatorium. She could not go to Hollywood, as it was too far from her high school. Like all young girls her age, school and her friends meant the world to her. So, as they had done since Laurie was born, Reeny, Frannie and their parents shared this child that belonged to them all. Brad came to accept there was something special about the relationship this family had with the darling child he came to love as his daughter. He sensed there were underlying currents of emotion surrounding Frannie and Reeny's love for Laurie. Instinctively he accepted his role in Laurie's life and tried to be the strong father figure he felt she needed. At the same time, he dealt with his love for his wife and his sorrow in her illness. He accepted he would not be a father to any child but Laurie. That was enough for him. He loved Laurie and he loved Reeny. As long as he could have them, that was all he needed to make him happy. He would give anything to be able to make Reeny whole and mentally healthy, but he could not do that. He was an excellent doctor in his own field, but the mind was something he did not pretend to heal. He stood by his wife and supported his family financially and emotionally as best he could. He was a quiet, gentle man, who took the good things life had to offer and tried not to be too adversely affected by the negative things life sent his way. He accepted the good times he had with his wife when she was well enough to be at home with him. When she became ill again, he stayed by her side as much as he could. Never once did he waiver in his devotion or his loyalty to Reeny. While he was mature enough to let Laurie go to Frannie's when she needed to, he also vigilantly maintained his role as Laurie's father. He faithfully traveled between Pasadena, Hollywood, and San Diego, trying to keep his small family as closely connected as these sad circumstances would permit. He was strong enough to let go of Laurie when he needed to so she could have some semblance of a normal childhood growing up at Frannie's house. Driving many miles with little sleep, he managed a tremendous balancing act, keeping Laurie in his life and Reeny's life both at their home and at the sanatorium. Through his maturity and kindness he kept the relationship alive between his wife and his daughter. He would not allow Laurie to drift off into a totally separate life in Hollywood. He knew Reeny loved her daughter, and it was not her fault she could not be the full-time mother most kids had while growing up. He sensed there was an extremely unusual bond between Reeny, Frannie, and Laurie. He did not question this closeness. He was grateful it existed. He could see Laurie was a part of both these sisters

Stephen and Emily loved to be with their cousin Laurie. When Laurie had her fifteenth birthday party, the whole family traveled to Pasadena to celebrate with her at Brad and Reeny's home. This was a good time for Reeny. With new drugs being developed, she had been able to stay at home for over a year now, with no trips back to the sanatorium. She and Brad were hopeful their life would be more normal now that she seemed to have her mental illness under control with a new regimen of various drug treatments. Philip, Frannie, Stephen and Emily piled out of their station wagon, all rushing to hug Laurie and wish her happy birthday. As Frannie watched this mature, serene teenager greet her guests, she realized how much she had missed Laurie this past year that she had returned home to her parents. Frannie had consoled herself with her very busy life of raising her son Stephen, who was eight years old, and his sister Emily, who was two years younger. She was too good of a person to begrudge her sister the same happiness she received from mothering her two young children. Astutely, she held her feelings for Laurie in check, becoming the doting auntie whenever Reeny took up her role as mother of Laurie. She was grateful for what Reeny had done for her fifteen years ago when she needed her to take care of Laurie. Frannie always stepped back when Reeny struggled to maintain her role as Laurie's mother. Like Brad, she knew it was not Reeny's fault she could not be the full-time mother she so desperately wanted to be.

Frannie accepted she would be required to mother Laurie on an as needed basis. She felt lucky to be given this chance to mother the child she had so long ago relinquished those rights to. It was a delicate balancing act, but because of her love for her sister and her daughter, she managed it. She felt blessed to have two other children she could lay claim to, and she never wanted to diminish Reeny's role as Laurie's mother. But now, watching Laurie, with the sunlight glimmering off her silver blonde hair, her heart swelled with love and pride. Always, she knew this girl would be hers. Share Laurie she would, but deep in her heart she looked at her with the proud eyes of a mother.

By the end of the evening, with the sun setting in the west, Emily was getting tired and whiny. The day had been perfect. Laurie had introduced them all to some new rock and roll songs. She even got her dad up and doing that new dance craze, the Twist. They had twisted and gyrated until Brad thought for sure he would throw his back out. Still, he would do anything to please his beautiful angel, who was so lovely but growing up much too fast. Stan and Stella remarked on how fast all three of their grandchildren were growing up. Laurie was a lovely teenager. Stephen was a handsome young boy. Their youngest granddaughter Emily was especially beautiful to look at. She was six years old. Unfortunately, her precocious personality put them all on edge. She was well-versed in throwing tantrums, screaming hysterically and putting many sets of teeth on edge. One had only to look at her dark gypsy eyes and lovely white skin, surrounded by her halo of curling black ringlets, and all was forgiven her. Emily was much too beautiful to stay mad at. The pleasure one received while looking at her was worth the cost of putting up with her behavior.

"Come here, you brat," laughed Laurie, as she gathered up Emily to put her in the car while Aunt Frannie gathered up Stephen and Uncle Phillip. After setting Emily safely in the back seat, Laurie closed the door as Aunt Frannie came up with Stephen.

Frannie hugged Laurie close as she said, "Laurie, I love you so much. Happy birthday, sweetheart. I am so happy you and your mom and dad are together. I hear you love high school. I miss you with all my heart, but I know you are happy to be with your mom and dad. I guess you know you have two families. We have always shared you, Laurie. No girl could be more loved than you. And now look at you, so grown up and beautiful." Frannie could not help a tear sliding down her cheek as she thought of when she had been Laurie's age. At fifteen she met Tim Slocum. Frannie thought how proud Tim would be of Laurie. Yet, of course, Tim knew nothing about Laurie. Sometimes Frannie wondered what became of Tim. She was certain he had done well for himself. He probably had lots of children and a wonderful wife. Deep down inside, Frannie felt tiny twinges of guilt over never letting Tim know this wonderful, beautiful girl was his. But it was far too late now for second thoughts. It was the 1960s and everyone's life was set in motion and moving forward.

From the house Reeny watched Laurie and Frannie as they said goodbye. Reeny had accepted there would be no more children in her life. It was strange how she never did conceive after her miscarriage. The doctor said she would be able to have other children, but she had never wanted to pursue the medical research into her inability to conceive. She did not want any secrets of Laurie's birth uncovered. No, she had accepted Laurie would be her only child, and she was grateful for the gift Frannie had given her so many years ago. She had control over her mental illness now, but deeply regretted missing out on those important years of Laurie's growing up. She reasoned it must be part of God's greater plan, this lifelong sharing of Laurie's life she and Frannie were caught up in.

She walked up to her daughter as she was waving goodbye to Frannie and Philip and the kids and she said to her, "Happy birthday, darling. I love you so much. No one could be luckier than I am having you as my daughter."

Laurie hugged her mother back, saying, "Thank you, Mom, I love you too. You're the best!" The two of them ran into the house and were met by Brad, who grabbed his two women gently by the arms and started to do the twist. Exhausted and out of breath, they all fell on the couch laughing at each other.

CHAPTER 20

Stan and Stella, along with a lot of other senior citizens, thought the whole world went crazy during the decade of the 1960s. Nothing was the same as it had been in previous decades. It started off sadly in the early part of the decade with the assassination of their beloved president, John F. Kennedy. Laurie was a senior in high school and the news shocked and devastated everyone. Yet, with the exuberance of youth, life went on. The Beatles arrived on American soil and quickly caused all teenagers and young adults to take leave of their senses. The country never saw such a frenzy of screaming, hysterical girls. Music exploded everywhere with a newness and uniqueness the older generations simply could not comprehend or appreciate. The newfangled transistor radios made it possible to tune into your favorite songs anytime and any place. Everywhere you went people walked around holding this small plastic box up to their ear while shaking and bouncing along, snapping their fingers in time to whatever song was playing on their transistor radio. It made the music mobile and teenagers loved it.

Laurie thought life was great as she approached her eighteenth birthday. The fashions were fantastic and daring. This generation was liberal. They were ready to show off their bodies. First came the two-piece swimsuit. The shock of seeing women's bellies in a swimsuit quickly gave way when the bikini came out. Everywhere you looked you saw skin. Miniskirts were great. Girls loved wearing them and men loved watching them. Legs were in. Thank goodness the nylon industry solved the problem of garters showing beneath miniskirts by inventing pantyhose. Woman thought the invention of pantyhose was the greatest scientific discovery of that decade.

Laurie was caught up in the wildness of the sixties. She loved the music, the fashions, and the overall freedom her generation had during this time. There was movement across the nation. America's youth jumped on Harleys or into Volkswagon vans and headed from the East Coast to the West Coast, stopping at all points in between. Young men and woman would sleep wherever they laid down their sleeping bags. People felt safe. Love was in the air. Everyone was your friend. It was the generation of the flower child, fully developed and ready to fly. The hippie movement had begun. Love, peace, and rock and roll was the theme of the sixties.

Unfortunately, onto this scene of newfound freedom and awareness came a source of trouble just beginning to unfold on this generation of young people. It came in the form of chemicals. While alcohol had always been around, this new source of chemical intoxication became know as dope. Drugs crept into the lives of the youth of the 1960s. Everyone was so caught up in experiencing new things and vowing to right all the wrongs of previous generations, they were caught unaware by the initial wave of chemicals landing in their midst. At first, thinking it experimental and harmless, it was the cool thing to do at this time. Marijuana made a welcome appearance and would stay for decades to follow. No one could begin to comprehend the trouble to come from this supposedly mind freeing substance the young people were so eager to try.

Brad, being a doctor, had some inkling of the beginning of trouble when young people began showing up in hospital emergency rooms experiencing horrors in their minds that only they could see. The myriad of chemicals young people were smoking, injecting, sniffing or swallowing produced a kaleidoscope of unreal images in their minds. Brad prayed it was a passing trend, but in his gut he knew it was not. Brad had no idea this insidious and dangerous pastime was creeping into his own beloved family.

"Come on, Laurie, try it. You just inhale some of it. It will make you feel so good," coaxed Sam. Laurie was afraid at first, yet everyone at the party was smoking pot and she didn't want to seem like a prude. After all, it was graduation. They had made it through high school and now it was time to celebrate. It did seem fun. So, without giving it anymore thought, Laurie reached over and took the joint from Sam. She took a drag and immediately started coughing.

She felt like her lungs were going to burst. She coughed so hard she had tears running down her cheeks. She passed the joint back to Sam, deciding it wasn't her thing to do. Sam took a long hit, and slowly breathed it out. His eyes were glassy and he smiled at Laurie. Laurie thought he was so cute, and she noticed the pot made his eyes look so beautiful, shiny, and bright. Feeling dreamy and very romantic towards Sam, Laurie took the joint again and tried inhaling a second time. This time, she got the hang of it and was able to hold the smoke in her lungs a few seconds before releasing it. After a couple times of doing this, she felt very lightheaded and detached, as if she were standing outside her own body watching herself and the other kids in the room. As she continued smoking pot with the other kids, it occurred to her that she was supposed to go home in a few hours. She wondered if she would come down by then. This was her first pot smoking experience and she was unsure how long the high was supposed to last. Lost in the haze of getting high, she put the consequences of her actions out of her mind for now and concentrated on getting high and having fun.

Several hours later she returned home. She crept up the stairs to her bedroom. She still felt dazed but was tired and relaxed now. Mom and Dad did not wait up for her and she thanked God for that favor. She felt almost normal now. She had only smoked one joint and was glad she stopped at one. She didn't like coming home stoned. She knew her parents would be very disappointed in her. She made a vow to talk with Sam tomorrow. She did not want to become a pot smoker. She liked her life the way it was. She was going on to college and so was Sam. She didn't want to take any chances messing up her mind now. Her brief experimentation with drugs was plenty for her.

Laurie went on to junior college for the next two years and Sam did the same. They smoked a little pot now and then, but for the most part concentrated on school. Laurie was going to UC Berkeley after she graduated from junior college and Sam was headed to UCLA. Laurie's life was fairly peaceful during these two years. Reeny was stable now. Brad didn't want her to return to work, so she became a homemaker and did volunteer work at the hospital in Pasadena. Brad was a great doctor and had established a good career at Pasadena Community Hospital. Stan and Stella remained living with Aunt Lil and Uncle Herb, so things were calm and quiet at the lovely big Victorian home.

Frannie and Philip kept busy with Stephen, who was entering his teen years, and their spitfire daughter, Emily. May's daughters had graduated college and were both married and lived near their mother in Hollywood. May had been working at the law firm since moving to California and had made a quiet life for herself with her lady friends. Now that her girls were married, she was constantly dropping hints about how wonderful it would be to become a grandmother. Laurie felt she would soon have some second cousins.

In 1965 Laurie turned twenty years old and graduated junior college. Reeny and Brad were very proud of their lovely, smart daughter. All the family showed up for Laurie's graduation party. Frannie and Philip came with Emily, who was twelve years old, and Stephen, a teenager now. Emily was as precocious as always and it was a darn good thing she was so cute, because one had to admit she was a brat. Laurie loved her and was the only one Emily really listened to. Emily was mature beyond her years. She acted like an adult. She didn't play well with children her own age, always adopting a superior, more grown up attitude. When all the family gathered, Laurie and Emily were inseparable. Laurie seemed to be the only person who understood Emily. Perhaps Laurie was more perceptive of Emily's feelings because she had grown up in two households herself, unsure where she really belonged. Laurie had grown up feeling like she had to justify and organize her love for her mother and Aunt Frannie. Laurie could be more sympathetic to the hard to understand Emily. Since it was easier, the adults let Laurie take over and were glad that Emily was close to Laurie and confided in her.

It was a great relief to Frannie. She tried so hard to be the perfect mother to Emily. She had no problem being close to Stephen. He talked to her. He opened up to her. They were close. But Emily treated her like she was the enemy. Emily wouldn't allow Frannie entrance into her thoughts or feelings. From the time she was a wee little girl, Emily had acted like Frannie was someone she had to tolerate because she was her mother. Laurie was the only adult Emily wasn't inherently suspicious of. Everyone kept saying Emily would take some hard knocks in life if she didn't get the chip off her shoulder. No matter how Emily acted, Laurie loved the little imp, and they shared a closeness that transcended their age difference. As Frannie watched her young daughter Emily stare adoringly at her cousin Laurie, she felt truly blessed. In her heart she was proud. These two girls were her daughters. She could lay claim openly only to one of them, but she knew they both had been born of her body.

Reeny came over and they stood together, arms around each other's waist. Reeny leaned over and whispered in Frannie's ear, "Thank you, Frannie, thank you for giving me, Laurie. I'm sorry I wasn't a better mother to her when I got sick. Thank you for giving her to me when she was born. Thank you for taking her back when I could not be there for her. I love you, Frannie. You are the most special person in the world to me."

Frannie hugged this older sister of hers that she loved very much. She whispered back to her, "Reeny, it's always been you and me. You said we would always be together and you were right. I love you with all my heart. We will stay close together. We will continue to watch Laurie grow and accomplish great things in her life. We will continue to share the girl we both love so much. She is ours, Reeny, and together we did a great job raising her. Thank you, Reeny, for making it possible to have Laurie in both our lives."

The two sisters walked arm in arm out into the large front yard of Brad and Reeny's spacious home. They stood together watching their parents, their spouses, Tom's sister May and her daughters and their spouses, Frannie's young children, Aunt Lil and Uncle Herb, and both felt truly blessed by a loving and forgiving God. So many years had passed since these two sisters bonded together to bring Laurie into this world as a loved and legitimate child. Laurie was the one secret they shared, yet so many other lives entwined with the life of this beautiful, young woman who was the centering force of these two sisters.

CHAPTER 21

Frannie admitted she had been a rebel as a teenager. Look at the trouble she had gotten into when she was just fifteen, unwed and pregnant with Laurie. She believed her problems resulted from feeling neglected due to all that was happening with her family and the terrible war at that time. She also had been extremely naïve about life and love. Now, more than twenty years later, things were coming back to haunt and mock her.

Another terrible war was being fought thousands of miles away in Vietnam and her precious Stephen was at risk of being drafted. She hoped and prayed he went straight on to college after he graduated in June, so hopefully he would not get drafted. That thought was much too frightening. Philip assured her he would do everything possible to keep Stephen out of the draft, but money could only protect them so much.

Then there was Emily. She was beautiful, sexy, and completely rebellious. Thank goodness Philip finally stepped up and took control. When Emily turned thirteen, things got really bad between her and Frannie. She had always been difficult, but at thirteen she was smart mouthed and disobedient. Finally, one night when the police brought Emily home drunk, Philip had had enough and took over. Severe discipline for the next two years had helped to control Emily, but there was no peace in the house when she was there. Just her presence in the home made Frannie sad. She could never understand why her daughter seemed to hate her so much. She loved Emily and was so proud of how beautiful she was. She tried so hard to be a good mother to Emily. She wanted to have a close relationship with her daughter, but it seemed as if Emily had thwarted her closeness from the very beginning. As a baby she was fussy and squirmed constantly when Frannie held her. Since Stephen was a toddler at the time, Frannie had been too busy to notice Emily's nature as a baby. Now, as she remembered things, she admitted Emily had always been a difficult child. Frannie considered herself a good mother to her two children. She was an easygoing woman. She could not comprehend why her own daughter seemed angry at the whole world at times. As Emily grew older, she became even meaner towards Frannie. It was only Philip's intervention and discipline that kept Emily from verbally abusing her own mother. Stephen's sweet nature kept Frannie from being devastated and consumed by Emily's meanness. Stephen tried so hard to compensate for Emily's hatefulness towards their mother. He was a well-behaved boy and tried hard to please both his parents. He considered his beautiful sister a brat, and at an early age began to keep his distance from her. Stephen was even-tempered and precise in his actions and temperament, but Emily could rattle his cage. She could get him angry like no one else could do. He was not a fighter by nature. When Emily was in one of her mean moods, she could anger him so much that inevitably they would end up in a squabble. Their bickering and fist fighting upset their mother. Sometimes, Stephen thought Emily picked fights with him just to upset their mother. Stephen loved his sweet mother and began to avoid close contact with his sister to keep from fighting with her. He wanted peace in his home. It was only when his father was at home that Emily behaved herself. His father put his foot down and demanded respect, politeness, and decent behavior from his errant daughter. Only Philip could control Emily, especially if she was in a particularly bad mood. As Emily grew older, her moodiness got more frequent and very ugly at times. She was rude to Stephen and her mother and both avoided her as much as possible.

For the first time in her life, Frannie was falling into despair. This despair was overwhelming and she did not feel she could climb out of it. It seemed to her as if her world was spinning out of control, and she could not grab onto it and hold it in the place she wanted it to be. She tried to take all the usual steps to keep her life organized and herself in control of her destiny. But factors outside her control were turning her life in directions she could not alter. In the last three years she had totally lost control of Emily. It was only Philip's strong discipline which kept Emily somewhat centered. Together, she and Philip had tried so many things to help them raise their strong-willed daughter. Although Philip left the majority of the child rearing responsibilities to Frannie, he realized Emily had emotional problems that required him to take a firm hand. He loved his beautiful, gypsy like daughter. But all his love could not protect Emily from her mistakes that resulted from her strong-willed personality. His daughter needed an active father figure in her life and he tried to be a good father. There was no appreciation or kindness in Emily. As a child she appeared cold, heartless, and self-absorbed. People who came into contact with their family could not comprehend how two such loving people as Philip and Frannie had produced what many called a bad seed. As Emily approached her sixteenth birthday, her behavior was a constant problem for Frannie and Philip. They simply tried to keep her out of trouble and in school until she could graduate high school. Philip promised to send her to art school in Europe if she did well enough in high school to get accepted at one of the European art schools in London or Paris. Frannie could not understand why Emily had to fight against everything in her life, when all she had to do was live by some very simple rules and the world would be her oyster. Her parents would do anything for her. To Frannie, Emily seemed bent on self-destruction, and she could not find a way to help her daughter. Every time Frannie tried to be part of Emily's life she was rudely and forcefully pushed away by Emily. She could not relinquish her parental duties, but that is what they became, duties. There was no joy in raising Emily. Frannie took the only route left to her. She gave Emily as much freedom as she dared to. She was trying to keep peace in the family, but at the same time keep Emily from ruining her life. These years were fraught with angry feelings, physical fights, and countless tears.

Stephen was her anchor in these dark times. She grew physically ill and mentally exhausted from fighting with Emily. Stephen kept his distance from his sister. Frannie was saddened to see her two children unable to form sibling bonds between themselves. Emily pushed everyone away from her. She wouldn't let anyone get close to her and she seemed to love no one. Laurie was at school in Berkeley and Reeny had returned to work at the hospital in Pasadena. Mom and Dad were retired and traveled around the country with Aunt Lil and Uncle Herb. The lovely, old Victorian home had long since been sold, and the four elderly folks had retired and bought homes in one of the new senior citizen neighborhoods. This was a time of rest for Mom and Dad. Frannie could not burden them with her problems about Emily. She was on her own now and she felt overwhelmed.

It was a cool October afternoon when Frannie was unpacking some warm sweaters for the winter when Stephen walked into the house. It was unusual for Stephen to be at home this time of the day. Frannie immediately got a sick feeling in the pit of her stomach. He walked up to her in the bedroom. He did not speak to her and had a serious look on his young, handsome face. Just looking into his soft brown eyes, she knew her baby was leaving. She sat down on her bed and Stephen sat down next to her. Taking his mother into his arms he told her, "Mom, I have been drafted. I managed to avoid it for a year now. But they finally drew my number. I've already been to the Army headquarters in Los Angeles and taken care of everything. I wanted to come home and spend the few days I have left here with you and Dad."

Frannie panicked. She kept asking Stephen how this had happened. Frannie thought he was safe from the draft. Frantically she said, "No, no, Stephen, you can't go to Vietnam. Too many young boys are dying over there. Our country is protesting that war. I thought you had a student deferment. Call your dad. He'll take care of everything. No, Stephen, you aren't going to Vietnam."

Calmly, Stephen unwrapped his mother's tightly clenched arms from around his shoulders. He looked down into beautiful brown eyes that were very much like his own as he said to her, "Yes, Mom, I am going to Vietnam. I can't stay here while so many other guys my age are going over there to fight for democracy. I can't let others go and do a job I must be involved in too. This is my country, and it needs me, and it's time for me to go."

Frannie felt like she had been transported back in time to when Reeny had told her about Tom leaving for the war in Europe. The words Tom had said to Reeny were almost identical to what Stephen was saying to her now. Into her frantically whirling mind came the words about history repeating itself and a great fear began to grow inside her. Numbly, she followed Stephen to his bedroom where he was going to organize his things and start packing his clothes. He had three days with his family before he had to report to Ft. Ord. Frannie, in a trance-like state, went to the telephone to call Philip at his office. After being put through to him by his secretary, she gave him the news about Stephen being drafted and asked him to come home.

She was resting on her bed in dazed misery when she heard Stephen and Philip shouting at each other. She got up and walked to Stephen's room, hearing Philip's scared voice saying to Stephen, "You can go to Canada, Stephen. I'm a lawyer. I will arrange things for you. There are thousands of young men going to Canada as conscientious objectors. Believe me, son, the war in Vietnam has plenty of opposition. So many people believe we should not be there. It cannot last much longer. There is too much dissension among the American people over this war. Stephen, you must go to Canada as a conscientious objector. We have enough money for you to live there until this horrible war is over, and then you can come back. They will have to eventually grant amnesty to the objectors in Canada. There are too many objectors up there not to let them return to their homeland. Trust me, Stephen, just go to Canada until it's over, and the government will let the objectors return. The American people are not sympathetic to the government anymore when it comes to Vietnam." Stephen let his dad go on talking, but he continued his packing. His face was set with determination. When his mother entered his room she was crying. He looked at her defeated face and realized his parents were getting older. His news had aged them within hours. He could see it in their desperate faces and slumped shoulders. It killed him to have to hurt and worry his parents. He felt he had to accept his draft number being called. He was not a superb student. He could not get excited about his education. His generation was torn apart by this war in Vietnam. Most of students he knew were confused about the war. It had been going on for several years. Tens of thousands of American GI's had been killed. Demonstrations were popping up all over the country. With the draft looming over his head during this year he had been attending the local city college, he never felt settled. He couldn't put his whole heart into school because he knew he would probably be drafted. He wanted to get it over with. He felt like he couldn't get on with his life until he went and did his duty and served his country. He knew his dad could probably get him safely to Canada, but he knew in his heart that was not the life for him. He had grown up hearing loving stories about Aunt Reeny's first husband, Tom, who had lost his life fighting for his country in Europe during World War II. He could not run, like a coward, up to Canada when someone in his own family had felt so strongly about fighting for American democracy. He was just glad he wasn't leaving behind a young pregnant wife like his Aunt Reeny had been back in the 1940s. Stephen had always loved and adored his beautiful Aunt Reeny. She was so loving and had been so sad much of his life. Somehow his Aunt Reeny's sadness had resulted in his cousin Laurie coming to live with them. Mom had explained to him how his Aunt Reeny had a sickness in her mind and that's why she was in the hospital so much. He loved his Aunt Reeny. She had always seemed so vulnerable to him, unlike his own mother who had a "take the bull by the horns" attitude with life. She was able to handle anything. Well, almost anything. She couldn't get a grip on his younger sister but then, who could? Emily was a totally different game. He loved her. Maybe he loved her because he was supposed to love her because she was his sister. He didn't question his love for Emily. She was his sister. He loved her. He didn't think she was a very nice person. He had learned from a young age to keep his distance from Emily. He always tried to keep peace in his family. It hurt him to see Emily upset his mom and dad so much. But there wasn't anything he could do about that. She was their kid and they would have to figure out how to raise her. With these thoughts of his family running through his head, he finished organizing his room, half listening to his father's pleas until finally his dad gave up and started helping him pack. They had three days together and he did not want to waste them arguing and watching his mother cry.

Frannie tried to be strong, but the overwhelming sadness at this time in her life threatened to consume her. For the first time ever, she wondered if this was how Reeny felt all those years when she could not hang on to a day's reality. It was like she was under water and could not breathe. She could not control the events in her life. They were whirling out of control, taking her children away from her. Stephen, who was now drafted into the Army, was leaving soon. Emily was lost in a world of anger and rebellion. Even Laurie was up in northern California at school in Berkeley. She hadn't written much lately and Frannie was worried about her. There was so much craziness in this generation of young people, Frannie was worried for them all.

CHAPTER 22

There was a reason Laurie had not written to Aunt Frannie for such a long time. She was tired of lying to her family. She had dropped out of college in June, just one year short of graduating. Her personal life was in such turmoil she could not concentrate on her studies. She was living with Bennie Nichols. He was a war protestor and a radical thinker who was determined to change the government's position on drugs and the Vietnam War. Part of Bennie's radical thinking was induced by mind-altering drugs. At first Laurie was agreeable to smoking pot and dropping acid, but Bennie wanted to reach greater spheres of conscious awareness. He was experimenting with stronger window pane acid, cocaine, and heroin. Instinctively, Laurie knew this was pushing the limit of what she considered acceptable drug experimentation. Laurie was deeply in love with Bennie and considered him informed, educated, brave, and a leader of men. She was becoming increasingly alarmed with Bennie's escalating interest in using drugs to expand his mind. He kept reassuring her he had control over using various drugs. He was experimenting. Their entire generation was experimenting, becoming more in tune with their surroundings. He encouraged her to try different drugs with him so they could stay together on the same level of awareness. Together they dropped acid and watched the wonders of the world parade through their minds while they had frantic, physically explosive sex. Laurie was so in love with Bennie she began to lose sight of her own personal self. Her intense love for him overwhelmed her common sense. It wasn't so much that she was interested in taking drugs herself. It was that she couldn't stand to be left behind when Bennie took drugs and went to some other realm of reality, leaving her behind in her straight world. For months she tried to accept his drug experimentation, tried not to let it bother her or make her feel like she wasn't part of his world. She tried to balance her love for Bennie, her dedication to school, and her mild experimentation with drugs.

As the months passed, Bennie and his friends stayed stoned most of the time. She stayed straight, trying to go to school and work. She felt so alone. Bennie was always partying with his friends. They would come over to her apartment. She would go into her room and try to sleep so she could go to school the next day. In the living room Bennie and his friends would drop the latest kind of acid and she could hear them talking and laughing. They tried to hold it down because they knew she was trying to sleep, but she was always uncomfortable knowing there was a living room full of hippies getting stoned while she tried to sleep.

She would go to school, day after day, while Bennie stayed home, getting stoned or smoking heroin. She would leave their apartment early in the morning, stepping over passed out people on the floor, many times stopping to cover up a naked couple too stoned to realize they had fallen asleep during intercourse. She felt she was losing a grip on what was important in her life. She loved him so much. She wanted to finish school, but it was becoming increasingly difficult to concentrate on her daily routine of work and school with all the craziness going on at home. She was no stranger to dabbling in drug use. She had started back in high school with the occasional pot smoking episodes with her then boyfriend, Sam. But life became more complicated as she grew older. She had too many goals to accomplish and could not afford the oblivion brought on by drugs. Some people, like Bennie, seemed to be able to go on with their daily routine even under the influence of drugs. She couldn't concentrate on school when she was stoned, so she tried to stay straight in the midst of all the craziness she was living in. It was like a huge wave she was fighting against, and she could feel herself being slowly sucked under that wave. She felt like such an outsider in her own apartment. She was the only one actively going to school. She had a part-time job that Bennie kept telling her she didn't need. He was selling kilos of marijuana and was making plenty of money. People were constantly in and out of their apartment all times of the day and night. This frightened Laurie. She was afraid they would get busted, but Bennie constantly assured her everything was fine, he had control of the situation. She had to admit he was making a lot of money. She chose to ignore that part of their life and pretend it did not exist. She relied on Bennie's judgement to keep them safe from the police. She immersed herself in school and tried to ignore the chaos growing in her personal life.

One evening she was in the kitchen doing her homework when she heard something land on the balcony outside the sliding glass door of the kitchen. She walked out onto the second story balcony deck and saw Bennie in the parking lot of the store next door to their apartment building. He was laughing and appeared to be wasted on something. Just as she was getting ready to yell down to him to get home and quit acting like a fool, she heard a loud knock on her front door. Her heart stopped and she experienced a sense of panic. Only the police would knock so loud and demanding. As she walked toward the door, she heard the dreaded words, "Police, open up." As she opened the door, four uniformed police officers burst into the apartment with a search warrant. She was the only one home and she prayed they would not look out the kitchen sliding glass door and see Bennie in the parking lot below. That prayer was short lived as two officers rushed past her yelling to their partners they were headed to the parking lot to get Bennie. With the other two officers watching her closely, she knew there was no way she could warn Bennie of what was going on in their apartment. She sat on the couch in the livingroom. She was getting sick to her stomach as she watched the officers pull suitcases of marijuana out of the closets and dump the pot into a big pile on the living room carpet, all the time exclaiming their excitement over this big drug bust.

Within minutes the other two officers returned to her apartment with Bennie in tow, securely handcuffed and being dragged between the two burly police officers. He looked at her with a dazed, glassy look in his eyes, as he said, "Hang in there, babe. I'll call my lawyer and he'll take care of everything. I've already told these guys you're completely innocent. You have nothing to do with this and they better leave you alone." But as Laurie looked at Bennie her heart sank. She saw immediately he was stoned on drugs and she could see the fear in his eyes. He tried to put on a brave face as he stood there handcuffed and unable to do anything to protect Laurie. Within minutes a female officer arrived and Laurie was handcuffed. Both she and Bennie were taken to jail where they stayed until Bennie's attorney bailed them out two days later.

After that arrest Laurie seemed to lose what little confidence she had left in herself. Her love for Bennie completely paralyzed her. She managed to get off with a light sentence of probation for living in the apartment where Bennie was selling marijuana. Bennie was sent to jail for a couple months, so Laurie moved in with Bennie's best friend until Bennie finished serving his time. During this time her life was peaceful. She couldn't concentrate on going to school, so she got a job at the local junior college working in the admissions office. She figured she needed this time to get her head straightened out and decide what to do with her life.

It was during this time that her cousin Stephen showed up in his army uniform to take her out to dinner. As she walked up to her apartment, she did not recognize the tall soldier standing on her front porch. As she got closer she saw Stephen's beautiful smile and his warm brown eyes, so like her own. She ran faster and soon she was swept up into Stephen's strong embrace. She had not realized how much she missed her family until this moment. Wiping away her tears she looked at Stephen and said, "God, it's wonderful to see you, Stephen. You are so grown up. I didn't know you were in the army." Laurie was ashamed of herself. Seeing Stephen in his uniform forced her to admit to herself that she had been so ashamed of the lifestyle she was living, she had cut off contact with her family. That is why she didn't know Stephen was in the service.

She could see concern for her in Stephen's eyes as he looked at her and said, "Yes, Uncle Sam finally got me. I'm over at Fort Ord in Gilroy for a couple more weeks. I had to come and see you. It's not too far from here. Laurie, we have all been worried about you. Why haven't you kept in touch with my mother? You know she loves you so much. And Emily, oh my god, you would not believe what a horrible brat Emily is. No one but you could ever control her. I have a million questions for you. Would you like to go to dinner with me? I'll quit talking long enough so we can go inside and you can grab a sweater. I'm starved, how about you?"

Laurie laughed as Stephen tried to fit years of catching up into this meeting on her front porch. As she unlocked the door and went to get her sweater, she assured him they had lots of catching up to do and would have plenty of time at dinner. This seemed to calm him down as they left the apartment and headed downtown to find a restaurant.

Later that evening, as they sat drinking iced tea and catching up on each other's lives, as well as all their relatives' lives, a peacefulness she had not felt in a long time descended on Laurie. Finally here was a link to her old, uncomplicated life. Back to a time before she began messing up everything good she had accomplished. But Laurie was an optimistic person and would not let her mistakes bury her. She tried to make Stephen understand her feelings for Bennie as she told him how much she loved him. To her it made sense, but Stephen was not looking convinced as she tried to justify her recent arrest record. She tried to explain what happened as she said, "Stephen, really it was just some pot. The cops made a big deal over Bennie selling some pot. Everyone smokes pot. He really should have gotten off with just probation, but the cops were out to make some kind of example out of him. Thank God I got off with probation. I don't think I could do jail time. I'm not tough enough to handle the jail scene. It scares me to think how close I came. I think Bennie has learned his lesson from this. When he gets out of jail, he'll get a job, and I can go back and finish school, and everything will turn out fine."

Stephen looked at his older cousin and wondered how someone so smart had so little common sense and was so gullible when it came to men. Just from what Laurie told him about Bennie, he could tell the guy was a loser, trying to get through life the easy way. But he kept his thoughts to himself. He could see Laurie was in love with this guy. Too bad, he thought, his cousin was in for a lot of heartache.

He tried to lighten the mood so they could end their time together on a happy note. Later that evening he dropped Laurie off at her place and headed back to Fort Ord to finish up boot camp. Right after that he was taking his thirty days leave before going to Vietnam. His mom was expecting him back in Hollywood to spend those thirty days with his family. He felt sad knowing he would have to tell his mom about his visit with Laurie. Damn, he wished he could protect these females in his family that he loved so much.

Several weeks after Stephen's visit, Bennie returned home to Laurie. She was aghast when Bennie got out of jail and immediately returned to getting high and selling drugs. For the past four months while Bennie was in jail, Laurie had led a quiet life, working and reading and waiting for Bennie to return so they could start out fresh. She had envisioned him getting a good job and her going back for her degree. It seemed to her from Bennie's attitude that he had just been waiting to get out of jail so he could resume right where he left off. Laurie was distraught. She tried to reason with him, begging him not to endanger them again, asking him over and over again if he loved her. He swore he did, but tried to make her understand this was the only way he could make good money. He made it perfectly clear he wasn't going to work for minimum wage at a dead end job. Why should he when he could get the best pot around town and knew all the connections to get it to the local street markets? He actually considered himself a business entrepreneur. Laurie had to admit he was a great salesman. Too bad his products were illegal drugs. Slowly Laurie accepted she wasn't going to change Bennie. She knew she wasn't going to be able to go back to school. Her life with Bennie was not conducive to studying or working. He maintained a lifestyle of people coming and going all hours of the night. Once again, Laurie was the straight chick, the outsider in Bennie's circle of cool friends. She wondered why he even wanted her as his girlfriend. As Bennie became a successful drug dealer, he was gone more and more, many times staying gone for days at a time. When he was home there was a constant parade of people, including beautiful young girls, coming in and out of their apartment. They all wanted to hang out with Bennie. He was good-looking, cool, and provided an unlimited supply of free drugs. It soon became obvious to Laurie that the girls swarming around Bennie were more than willing to spread their legs in exchange for a free high. It disgusted her, the lifestyle she and Bennie had fallen into. Bennie loved it. He had attention from his peers, sexy girls, and groupies fawning over him for his attention and free drugs. Laurie could not combat this lifestyle Bennie chose to live, nor could she find the strength within herself to leave him. Slowly she too began to experiment with different drugs, trying to ease the pain and guilt that was consuming her as her life spiraled out of her control.

CHAPTER 23

Frannie drove to Pasadena determined to make Reeny accept the reality of what was happening to Laurie. It had been several months since Stephen came home on leave and told her how worried he was about Laurie and the lifestyle she was living. Frannie had called and begged Laurie to come home. She knew things were bad in Laurie's life. She could hear the fear and despair in Laurie's voice. She knew she must be the strong one. Reeny's mind was fragile. She kept her sanity only by concentrating on a daily basis. New prescriptions had enabled her to live at home now for years, but you had to tiptoe around Reeny. Brad was very protective of Reeny. He was always worried something would put her over the edge and send her back to the sanatorium. Frannie was angry and felt Brad and Reeny should be more forceful with their daughter, or at least quit burying their head in the sand. They needed to see that Laurie was in trouble and not able to save herself.

Frannie slammed the car door and ran up the front steps. She pounded her fists loudly on the door yelling for Reeny. As Reeny opened the door Frannie said, "Reeny, things are not good with Laurie. We have to go up north and get her. I'm worried sick about her. Stephen told me a lot of things about Laurie and that guy Bennie she lives with. Reeny, did you know Laurie got busted and was in jail? I don't think she is even going to school. Reeny, our Laurie needs us. I can feel it. She is in trouble."

As Reeny ushered her distraught sister into her kitchen, she tried to calm her down, saying, "Alright, Frannie, we will look into the situation. But calm down. I'm sure you're exaggerating things. I get letters from Laurie. She sounds fine. She is working and had to put school on hold for awhile. She said she couldn't focus on studying right now, but she assured me she would return to school next year. She's young. She can take a year off if she needs to. What's this about her being arrested? She never said anything about that to me. Are you sure Stephen has his facts correct?"

Frannie could not believe her sister was living in such a rose-colored world. For the first time in her life she was angry with Reeny and it came out in her voice as she said, "Wake up and smell the coffee, Reeny. Laurie is lying to you. She went to jail for a couple days and is now on probation for five years. That jerk she lives with is a drug dealer and he went to jail for several months. He got out again and has gone right back to dealing drugs. I'm telling you, Reeny, it's just a matter of time before they're both busted again. Laurie's head is all messed up. She thinks she's in love with this guy and she's too confused to get herself out of the whole mess. We have to go up there, Reeny, and we have to go now."

This news seemed to age Reeny overnight. After Frannie left and went back to Hollywood, Reeny called Brad at the hospital and asked him to come home after his shift. They needed to talk about Laurie. She told Brad everything Frannie had told her. Brad's first reaction was the same as Reeny's. They wanted to believe Frannie was exaggerating. They could not believe their lovely, smart daughter had gotten herself into such a tragic situation. The only nagging doubt was that they knew their daughter was so gullible, so loving, such a romantic. If her heart was tied to this guy then her head may be all mixed-up with her emotions. They knew how loving and good their daughter was, and they were afraid this guy could easily use and manipulate her through the love she had for him. Rather than run up north, Brad and Reeny decided to wait awhile. After all, Laurie was twenty-five years old, a grown woman. She did not have to do anything she didn't want to do. They could not force her to return to Pasadena.

Frannie was furious at Brad and Reeny's choice of direction. She felt they should go right up north and fetch their daughter home. Reeny repeatedly told Frannie that Laurie assured her everything was alright. Sure, Laurie's life wasn't perfect, but she was doing okay and didn't want Reeny's interference.

One afternoon, Reeny and Frannie sat in Frannie's house in

Hollywood. Reeny had driven up to see her sister to try to mend fences. Reeny implored Frannie to understand as she said to her, "Please, Frannie, you must realize Laurie is twenty-five years old. I can't make her do anything. My God, Frannie, if anyone should understand it should be you. Emily is only seventeen years old and you have never been able to get that girl to do anything she doesn't want to do. If Philip didn't threaten her daily that child would have been in juvenile hall years ago. Don't get me wrong, I love Emily and have always thought you a saint of a mother. She doesn't deserve you. Oh, I know Emily would have put me back in the looney bin years ago. But the point I'm trying to make is, we can't force these children of ours, especially our adult children, to live their lives the way we want them to. They have to make their own mistakes. It breaks my heart, thinking Laurie is unhappy. I want her life to be perfect. I wished it were possible to buy her happiness, anything to make her happy, but I can't do that. She won't let me. She has to find her own way. Maybe because of all those years I was in the sanatorium while she was growing up, she is afraid to burden me with her problems. Maybe she thinks if she opens up to me, it will be too much for me to handle. Maybe she is afraid I will go back to the sanatorium. Frannie, I swear, I have told her I am so much stronger now. There is medication for me now that was never available when Laurie was a little girl. I've begged her to tell me if she is in trouble. I can handle it now. I can be a mother to her. I can be there for her if she needs me. Frannie, she repeatedly tells me she can handle her own life. She actually got mad at me the last time I called to check on her. She told me to mind my own business and leave her alone. That hurt me badly. What more can I do if she insists on maintaining the illusion that her life is fine?"

By this time Reeny was in tears, consumed with guilt over the past, her inability to raise Laurie when she was young, and her inability to fix Laurie's life now. Frannie could not bear to see her sister so devastated. She pulled Reeny into her arms and tried to console her. Deep in her heart she knew Laurie was in trouble, but it was easier to accept Reeny's explanation of things and quit worrying for the moment. Somewhere in her mind she knew she would have to go and see for herself what was happening with Laurie, but for now she left it alone. She had to accept Reeny's decision to wait and see for the time being. Reeny and Frannie sat together in Frannie's home in the Hollywood Hills for the rest of the afternoon. They enjoyed their peaceful time together, discussing their children. They talked about Laurie, trying to put an optimistic band-aid on her current living situation. They talked about Stephen and their constant prayers for him and the other soldiers in Vietnam. Finally, they talked about Emily. Reeny apologized for any unkind remarks she had made about Emily earlier in the day. Because they had no other choice, they both reassured each other their children would turn out alright somehow, someway. As the afternoon sun began to filter in through the western windows of Frannie's home, Reeny started to think about her drive back to Pasadena. She kept postponing her departure. For some reason unknown to her, she felt drawn to stay in the house with Frannie.

CHAPTER 24

The shrill of the phone caused both sisters to jump. So consumed with their worry over Laurie, they were oblivious to the outside world. Frannie picked up the phone to hear Philip's voice on the line. Something was wrong with his voice. Her stomach turned over and she could not breathe. For some reason, Philip tried to sound normal. He said he was checking to see if she was home. He needed to come home and talk to her. No, he couldn't discuss it now. He would be home within the hour. Instinct told her not to ask any more questions.

Lost in a temporary state of fearful anticipation, Frannie waited for Philip to arrive. Reeny could see the color drain from Frannie's face as she replaced the receiver of the phone in the cradle. Both sisters looked at each other and suddenly they were transported back to that awful time so many years ago when they learned their beloved Tom would not be returning from Europe. But Frannie refused to let that thought formulate in her mind. No, no, she must be calm. It was probably just Philip's health bothering him. He hadn't been feeling up to par lately. He was having problems with his cholesterol and high blood pressure. The doctor was trying him on different medications. That must be his problem. For just a moment, she was relieved, thinking it must be Philip she had to worry about. She was sure Stephen was fine. Letters from him in Vietnam were fairly consistent. They came about once a month. He didn't say much. He seemed depressed with all the horror he was witnessing there, but he only had a few more months until his year-long tour of duty would be finished. With that reassurance firmly in her mind, she puttered around the kitchen for the next hour waiting for Phillip.

Reeny was scared. Her heart was beating faster than normal. She did not like to think about all the hurt she had suffered in the past. She was not a mentally strong person like her sister Frannie. She lived with guilt almost daily. She was constantly in therapy dealing with

137

her past demons, her chemical imbalances, her mental illness, and her tenuous grasp on reality. Many days Reeny hung onto her sanity by a thread. Instinct told her that thread better be strong today. Her sister, Frannie, was the strong one. She prayed that God would not let anything happen to hurt Frannie. Frannie was the one who kept the family functioning in one way or another. Reeny leaned on her constantly. Reeny felt she had failed her sister in raising Laurie. The truth was that after Reeny had her nervous breakdown, Frannie had finished raising Laurie. Reeny admitted she couldn't handle much herself and prayed that God would spare Frannie any devastating news.

Philip walked into the kitchen. Immediately Frannie knew the worst had happened. In her panic she reasoned that if she didn't hear anything then nothing bad could be told to her. All she knew was she was screaming uncontrollably as she fell down this long dark tunnel, falling and screaming, all alone down this long black pipeline until she fell into oblivion. Frannie remained in this cocoon of mental safety all during the time Philip made arrangements to receive Stephen's body from Army personnel. She made incoherent motions of helping Philip make funeral arrangements for their beloved young son. The entire family was stunned. To Mom, Dad, Reeny and Frannie, it was déjà vu from the horrible days they had endured while tending to Tom's burial. Even May was racked by the sadness of Stephen's death, bringing the loss of her brother into the present, all the pain and agony of his death relived again with Stephen's death. Added to the pain of Stephen's death was the country's attitude towards the Vietnam war. The country did not have its usual patriotic attitude towards its fighting soldiers. Always before, in times of war, America encouraged and appreciated the soldiers who gave their lives fighting for freedom and democracy. The Vietnam war generated an attitude of indifference among the country's population. There was so much dissension and demonstration over the righteous of this war. But to Stephen's family, what difference did it make, whether American should or should not be involved in Vietnam. The fact was that American was involved. Stephen was involved and now Stephen was dead. Once again this brave family, grown larger now, stood beside a flag draped coffin. Sadly they listened to the twenty-one gun salute and watched another fallen soldier enter eternal rest. Once more a white orchid, freshly gown in warm Californian sunshine, dropped onto the dark grains of earth covering Stephen's coffin as it slowly descended into the ground.

After Stephen's death Frannie's strong personality withered. She had a hopeless, despairing attitude. She no longer cared what Emily did. Emily's outrageous behavior did not affect her anymore. The girl was only seventeen years old and her mother was done raising her. As far as Frannie was concerned, Emily could do whatever she wanted to. The fight had gone out of Frannie. Philip tried to keep his family functioning together. His beautiful young daughter seemed hell bent on having a constant good time. Her life revolved around her friends and parties. She attended high school only because her father threatened to make her life a living hell if she did not graduate. She made a perfunctory effort at school. It was only her genetic intelligence and high IQ that kept her doing well in high school. Her father knew Emily could be a great scholar if she would only apply herself. Emily was extremely artistic and Philip believed she had great talent. He tried to tempt her, offering to send her to art school at the Sorbonne Institute if she would just make the grades. Surprising everyone in her family, as well as her friends, Emily did buckle down her senior year. At last Philip breathed a sigh of relief. His beautiful, talented, headstrong daughter was finally showing some signs of maturity. Finally, to everyone's relief, Emily finished her senior year of high school. At her graduation her family gathered around, congratulating her on good grades and the valiant effort she made to graduate. Everyone except Stephen was there. His absence was like a knife thrust deep into Frannie's heart. She went through the motions of living but felt like one of those robots in that new movie about Stepford wives. Many times she wondered if it had been this bad for Reeny when she lost Tom. She didn't think so. She thought losing a child must be the most horrible trauma any human being could experience. She didn't feel alive, but she knew she wasn't dead yet. She lived in a suspended state of merely existing. She woke up every morning and wondered why she was still alive. It seemed to her that she lived only because she had no other choice. Somehow, since Stephen's death, Emily and Philip had reached some kind of understanding. They both realized Frannie had detached herself from them and they only had each other. Perhaps this was a good thing for Emily. It forced her to grow up and take some responsibility for her own actions. Nothing else had worked. Not Frannie's hysterical screaming or Philip's constant threats of punishment had ever, even minutely, altered their errant daughter's behavior. Yet, in this past year, she had grown up. She graduated with honors and even earned an art scholarship. Perhaps Emily realized she had lost her brother and was in the midst of losing her mother, if only mentally and emotionally. Emily had always been the detached one, acting as if she needed no one but herself. Perhaps the realization that she may end up with just herself scared her and forced her to admit some vulnerability on her part. She reached out to Philip, and the two of them formed a tenuous bond as Emily moved forward with her life and out of the secure fold of her home.

After graduating from high school, Emily stayed with her family for her summer vacation. At the end of summer she took her father up on his promise to help her get an artist's education in France. Combined with her scholarship and her father's help, Emily left for school in France at the end of summer. Although Frannie was still silent and withdrawn a year after Stephen's death, she was beginning to come back to this world. She was proud of her daughter and they had reached a truce. Never very close, they were at least polite to each other that day when Emily flew out of Los Angeles Airport for the sixteen hour flight to Paris. Frannie was thankful her daughter had matured and seemed to be finding some inner peace within herself. She knew Emily had great talent. If she painted with the same exuberance she lived her life with, she would be a great success.

CHAPTER 25

The house seemed so quiet after Emily left for France. Frannie wandered through her modern, immaculate home she and Philip had built so many years ago. She wondered where the years had gone. If Stephen were still alive he would twenty-one years old. Her heart ached for her son and his lost life. They were well into the beginning of the 1970s. For the first time in her life Frannie felt unfocused. She felt lost with no direction or purpose. Her son was dead. She never had a strong bond with Emily, and now Emily was gone from her life, if only temporarily. In certain ways even Philip had left her. He had his law practice to consume him. He had his work as his emotional outlet. He seemed to be working all the time now. Frannie couldn't blame him. She didn't want to be here in this silent home, wandering through its big, beautifully decorated rooms, so chic it did not even feel comfortable anymore. With Philip's success mounting each year, he had lavished material wealth on his family in the form of this beautiful home and all the furnishings within it. But this house meant nothing to Frannie without children in it to give some life to the structure. Her depression mounted as she wandered through her beautiful, sunny home that early fall morning, wondering what she would do to occupy her time throughout the long days ahead.

She could barely watch the news anymore. All those tens of thousands of young boys killed in Vietnam. Her own beautiful son was dead and gone. Now the United States was pulling their soldiers out of Vietnam. It was like the country was giving up. What a waste of human lives. She wanted to throw up so great was her distress when she thought of Stephen. She remembered her futile wishing that she had forced him to go to Canada. Soon all those draft dodgers would be granted amnesty by the government and they would return home. Her Stephen wasn't returning home, not ever. She felt so helpless, so remiss as a mother. She sank lower and lower into her depression as she chastised herself for failing Laurie. She was unable to acknowledge she was Laurie's mother. She thought of Stephen and she felt she had not protected him from a vile, senseless war. She thought of her daughter Emily. That girl was so indifferent to Frannie, it was hard for her to believe she had actually come from her womb. Frannie sat there in her den. She was unable to move. She was distraught in her agony over the loss of her son and her feelings of failure.

The ringing of the doorbell was insistent. Whoever was pushing it was relentless in the frantic repeating of the chimes. "I'm coming, I'm coming, hold on a moment," yelled Frannie, as she ran through the house to the front door. It took a few seconds to run through the large, spacious home to the front door. She was out of breath as she pulled open the double mahogany doors. "Oh my God" was all she could say as she looked into Laurie's gaunt, troubled face. Frannie quickly recovered her wits and drew Laurie into her arms, feeling the sharp angles of her bones as she held her closely. Laurie simply laid her head on her Aunt Frannie's shoulder and began to weep like a little girl as Frannie drew her inside and shut the door to the outside world.

"Brad, you need to come right over. She's in pretty bad shape. I've put her to bed, but she is throwing up, shaking, sweating. And, Brad, there's something else I must tell you. She has obviously been using drugs. There are horrible bruises and scabs on the inside of both her arms. Please, Brad, hurry, she's sick. I'm scared. Please don't let us lose her, Brad. You decide about Reeny, whether you want her to know everything now or wait awhile. I know she's been having bad spells lately with her mood swings. I'll leave that decision to you, but for now, please get here as soon as you can," begged Frannie as she replaced the telephone receiver into its cradle. She walked back into the guest bedroom where she had put Laurie to bed and watched her daughter suffer as she twitched and moaned in a restless, fitful sleep. Her guilt feelings nearly crippled her. She couldn't even use Stephen's death as an excuse for ignoring Laurie's desperate plight. Right before Stephen died she had known Laurie was in trouble. When Stephen died she stopped being a mother to anyone. It was easier to pretend Laurie had figured out her own problems. It had been easier to listen to Reeny telling her everything was alright with Laurie when deep inside Frannie knew this was not true. It was easier to ignore Emily. She had let Philip take over while she hoped for the best without having to actively participate. She had crawled under her blanket of grief, ignoring everyone, content to lie there with her wounded heart. As she watched her child suffer, her remorse was so great it suffocated her. But she refused to let her emotions overwhelm her anymore. She had to get strong. For over a year now she had catered to her emotional needs, letting them absorb her every waking moment. No more, no more! Finally she had to put Stephen's death behind her and get on with living. She would not lose another child.

Brad arrived and Frannie quickly led him to see Laurie. By this time, Laurie was delirious, crying and screaming at demons only she saw. Brad had not told Reeny anything yet about Laurie's return. He wanted to see Laurie first and assess the situation before bringing Reeny to see her. Brad stopped and looked down at his suffering daughter. He fell to his knees as he cradled Laurie in his arms and openly wept as he held her and cried out in anguish, "Laurie, Laurie, Daddy's here now. I am so sorry. Please forgive me, Laurie, for not being with you when you needed me. I'm here now and I am going to make you well again. I will never let you be alone again. I will always be with you. I love you, Laurie, I love you." Brad's sobs shook his entire body as he held his precious daughter in his arms.

Brad put Laurie in a private hospital later that day. After his emotional reunion with his beloved daughter, he was quick to see Laurie was very ill. Undoubtedly, she was heavily addicted to some drug. She wasn't coherent enough to tell him. He knew Laurie's medical and emotional ills, as well as her acute drug addiction, were beyond his professional expertise. He contacted his associates and quietly put Laurie where she would get the best care. After getting her safely settled into Chapters Rehabilitation Hospital, he drove back to Pasadena to deliver the news of Laurie's return to Reeny.

For the time being he felt it was better to leave Laurie in Hollywood. She would be close to Frannie, who was at her bedside constantly. He did not know if Reeny could endure the emotional upheaval of dealing with Laurie's problems right now, but he had to tell her. He prayed Reeny could handle the upcoming battle of helping Laurie get back to the way she was before she moved to Berkeley. He had very little information on the last couple years of Laurie's life. Slowly, over these past two years she had receded from them. She maintained very little contact with any of her family. Stephen had visited her when he was up at Ft. Ord. Stephen had been concerned about Laurie then. Brad remembered Reeny and Frannie taking steps to contact Laurie and find out what was going on in her life. Brad had gotten the impression that Laurie was alright. At least that was what Frannie and Reeny had indicated to him. When Stephen died Laurie had come down for the funeral. She looked a bit thin and pale, but he had attributed that to the current fashion trend of being thin. God, he had been a fool! Why hadn't he paid more attention to his daughter? He had been immersed in his professional career, consumed with caring for his mentally ill wife, and somehow Laurie had slipped through the cracks. He would never forgive himself. Always, Laurie had been the victim. All those years when she had lived with Frannie, he was torn between caring for his sick wife and trying to be a decent father to Laurie. Even then he had let Frannie and Philip take over what should have been his job of raising Laurie. He begged God for another chance to make it up to Laurie. As he made that agonizing drive from Hollywood to Pasadena, he felt he was at his lowest point ever in his life. What had he accomplished in his life if he had failed his daughter? Her biological father had died before she was born and her mother was mentally ill. He should have been the strong anchor in Laurie's life and he had failed her. God had given him this little girl to cherish and care for and he had not done a decent job raising her. The years went by so fast and there was always so much happening in their lives. He always meant to spend more time with Laurie but somehow the time had gone by. As he looked back over the years, it seemed like only yesterday when

Laurie had been a beautiful little girl with her silver blonde hair and big brown eyes staring up at him and calling him her new daddy. He thought he would die from the guilt and pain in his heart.

"I will leave first thing in the morning. You come up when you can. I will stay with Frannie and Philip," said Reeny calmly as she packed her suitcase. Brad had expected tears, recriminations or hysterics. He had expected anything other than this calm attitude of Reeny's. What he did not know was that Reeny knew she had to stay calm. Her child was in danger and needed her. It was imperative Reeny stay sane. She could not lapse into being an emotional cripple now. Her daughter needed her to be strong and she vowed to be the mother Laurie needed her to be. She had known something was wrong in Laurie's life. She had kept much of her knowledge hidden from Brad. Laurie refused to let her intervene. Through the years, as Reeny tried to get into Laurie's life to help her, she could feel Laurie pushing her back. Finally, she had been forced to withdraw her intrusion into Laurie's life, afraid of being ostracized completely by Laurie. She had hung on to a thread keeping her minimally connected to Laurie. An occasional phone call had to sustain her. At least she knew Laurie was surviving. If she pushed harder she knew instinctively Laurie would be lost to her. Her prayer was Laurie would pull herself out of whatever dark abyss she was falling into. She had a thin link to Laurie and she prayed it would be enough if Laurie needed her. Not once during this time of being pushed out of Laurie's life did Reeny not think of her beloved daughter. She knew from infrequent phone calls that Laurie still held on to that tenuous connection to her mother. It was imperative that fragile connection not be severed. Now Laurie had pulled on that connection and Reeny would reel herself back into her daughter's life and help her.

CHAPTER 26

Six months later, Laurie's family watched her speak at the podium, describing her life as a drug addict. Never would anyone have thought such a thing could happen to Laurie. She had been such a perfect little girl. She was so smart, well-behaved and beautiful. Those kinds of girls did not become drug addicts. They went on to college, became beauty queens, and married successful men. This disease mystified both Reeny and Frannie. After their initial shock, they both learned everything they could about this horrible disease affecting a large segment of America's youth. Drugs had taken the country by storm during the 1960s and their use continued rampantly throughout the 1970s. No one was safe, and society was just beginning to feel the repercussions of this disease. Recovery was still a fairly new concept. Most people still felt drug addicts were hopeless lowlifes who belonged in prison or mental hospitals. Laurie's survival of this episode of her life was nothing short of a miracle. She held on tight to her recovery. She knew she was a doomed woman without it. Wedged behind the podium with her pregnant stomach protruding, she thanked her higher power for saving her life and that of her unborn child. Those first few weeks after she came home, she had been so sick from detoxing off heroin, she thought she would die. Compounded with her addiction, she was pregnant. The doctors thought she might lose the baby during her detoxification period. She had been too sick to care about anything, not her own life or her baby's life. Her mother and Aunt Frannie had stayed by her side constantly until she was out of danger. She was only beginning to work through the emotional quagmire that surrounded her mental inabilities to cope with life. She had suffered much in these early months of recovery but never once did she feel sorry for herself. It was taking her a long time to forgive herself for what she had done to herself. With the help of her counselors, her peers, and her family, she began to believe she could continue on with her life. She had broken all ties with Bennie. He knew she carried his child, but he wasn't interested in her or the baby. He had moved on, farther north to Oregon where he had organized a group of people on a commune up in the mountains. Laurie had finally realized Bennie considered himself a guru of sorts. He loved bending people's mind to his own way of thinking. Perhaps if he had channeled his talents in other directions he would have made a great professor, so intense was his influence with people. Unfortunately, somewhere along the way, drugs had taken control of him, and his influencing could lead down dangerous paths. Laurie had experienced his dangerous influence firsthand and was thankful she had gotten away from him alive. Her heart was battered. He had been a great love in her life. She was older now and without the influence of drugs she could see their love was tainted by their drug use. She and Bennie had never had a totally straight, drug free relationship. Their love for each other was distorted by their drug use. Eventually, her memories of her love for Bennie began to fade and her heart began to heal as she waited for the birth of her child.

Laurie had moved home with Reeny and Brad after she left the rehab hospital. Soon after she moved home she went back to school. She enrolled at UCLA and finished her studies. That summer, her whole family was there to watch her walk across the platform to get her degree. Finally, she finished college. Her black graduation robe barely covered her huge stomach. Her baby was due any time now. It had been a turbulent nine months. She had beaten her addiction, hanging on everyday to her inner strength, ever mindful of any temptations or emotional upheavals that could threaten her sobriety. Her mother had been an unbelievable source of strength to Laurie during this time. She never chastised or lectured Laurie on her past mistakes. Never once was Reeny's mental stability threatened. Laurie had been afraid her problems would be too much for her mother to handle and would drive her back to her struggle with mental illness. But, partly due to all the new medication, Reeny had been fine. She stood steadfastly by her daughter, never once wavering in her help. She went to recovery meetings every night with Laurie for months at a time. She was up many nights with Laurie as her daughter sobbed out her heartache, regret, and shame over the past few years of her life. Reeny remembered her own experiences with the demons of her mind. She battled a constant fight against mental illness. Suffering a disease herself, she could well sympathize with Laurie in her fight against her drug addiction. Mother and daughter needed each other during this time. A new, mature bond between these two adult women was formed. As Laurie grew bigger in her pregnancy, a contented happiness settled on Laurie and Reeny. For many years Reeny had been unable to mother a young Laurie. Both women had endured their separation in Laurie's early twenties. Now, as everyday brought them closer together, mother and daughter found their way back to each other and languished in the love they had for each other.

"Breathe, Laurie, breathe," commanded Reeny, as her daughter struggled with her contractions. The doctor ordered Laurie to quit pushing. It was not time yet. She wasn't fully dilated. For just an instant Reeny grew fearful. She was remembering a time so long ago when she had lost her baby. But that was a lifetime ago. Through her years of living that sorrow had lost its intensity. She had come a long way and had lived through great sorrows. For many years her mind had hidden from these emotions, unable to digest correctly the stimuli exchanging between her heart and mind. During those years she had been forced to take refuge in hospitals and sanatoriums, protected from emotions she could not interact with. Now, finally, she could face life on its own terms. She found her way back to living and discovered great joy in her everyday life. She had help. She had the love of a wonderful man who stood by her through everything life dealt them. She had the benefit of modern day medical miracles with medications to help control mental illness. She had her beautiful daughter back in her life. And now she had the added joy of a grandson. Just moments ago, Benjamin Stephen St. Clair-Nichols was born. Reeny looked over and saw Frannie holding the newborn baby, tears of happiness running down her cheeks. Silently she watched her younger sister whom she loved so much. Always, life kept them together sharing in their love for Laurie. She was the child they had shared now for over twenty-six years. Their eyes met and a loving look passed between these two middle-aged sisters. Once again, they had a baby to share, a grandson.

Having Ben in their lives brought youth back to Frannie, Philip, Reeny and Brad. This little boy warmed the hearts and brought joy to the souls of these middle-aged grandparents and great aunt and uncle. Having Ben to love helped them heal from their loss of Stephen. Cheated out of sharing Stephen's life by his young death, they had renewed hope for the future in Ben. Laurie wanted to name the baby boy Benjamin after his biological father and Stephen after her beloved cousin who had died in Vietnam. Laurie knew her son would never know his father. She wanted to give him his father's name so he would have something of the man who had created him.

By the time Ben was getting ready to enter preschool at age four, his life was full of love. He lived with his mother, who was a teacher at Pasadena Junior College, and his grandparents. His grandmother took care of him while his mother taught school. His great aunt Frannie came often from Hollywood and he loved her visits. They were always special, and Aunt Frannie took him to fun places, like the LA Zoo and the La Brea Tar Pits. Ben never lacked for attention. He had plenty adults in his life, and he never mentioned not having a father. He may notice this later as he got older. For now Ben's life was full of love and joy.

CHAPTER 27

It was a lazy Saturday afternoon and Laurie and Reeny were reading in the cozy den in their home in Pasadena. Brad had taken Ben to the park to play baseball. Reeny glanced over and saw a huge purple bruise on Laurie's upper arm. Alarmed, she got up from where she sat and walked over to stand in front of Laurie. "Laurie, you have to be more careful. You have another bruise on your arm. Did you run into something?" asked Reeny, as she rubbed her daughter's arm. "You better go see your dad, maybe you're becoming anemic. You seem to bruise quite easily lately," said Reeny, as she shot her daughter a concerned look. Reeny was just past fifty years old. Since Laurie's return home, she doted on both Laurie and Ben. Laurie constantly told her to quit smothering Ben and let him be a little boy. Dad was a doctor. He wouldn't let anything happen to Ben. Laurie gave her mother that 'you're being overprotective' look. but was immediately contrite when she saw the sad, dejected look appear on Reeny's face.

"Oh, Mom, I'm sorry. I didn't realize you were so worried about me. Of course, I'll have Dad run some blood tests. I have been feeling a little tired lately. I'm sure I'm just burning the candle at both ends. Going back for another master's degree may be taking on a bit too much. Teaching all day and taking night classes may be more than I can handle right now. But we'll see. I'll call Dad's office and make an appointment,"said Laurie soothingly. She saw the relief register immediately on Reeny's face.

Reeny and Laurie had developed a wonderful bond between themselves. Frannie also formed part of that bond. As Reeny reflected over the years, she realized it had always been the three of them, Reeny, Frannie, and Laurie. Other lives and loves came along. Each relationship had its own set of sorrows and joys. Reeny saw that no matter what happened in their lives, she and Frannie had always shared Laurie.

As Reeny sat there musing over her life, she began to miss her sister. Frannie had gone to France to visit Emily. It had been a sudden decision and as yet Reeny was not sure why Frannie had rushed over to France with no advance notice to anyone. The first Reeny knew of the trip was when Frannie asked for a ride to the airport. Reeny wished that Frannie's daughter Emily would come home for a visit. Laurie missed her cousin Emily and Emily had never seen little Ben. Emily was very busy in Paris. In her mid-twenties, she was a hugely successful artist. Her paintings had decadent price tags and she maintained a high dollar gallery in MonteMarte. Reeny reflected on what a difficult child Emily had been. She had been such a beautiful little girl. She took after Philip in looks. She had curly black hair and dark green eyes with long black eyelashes. She had a little pointed, elfish looking face and full red lips. All in all, she looked exactly like a gypsy. There was fire in her eyes and fire in her spirit. She was meant to be a painter. Her exotic looks combined with her fiery nature, bohemian values, and great talent all made Emily the great artist she had become. Reeny could tell Frannie missed her daughter. They had lived on different continents for years now without seeing one another. Frannie and Emily had never been close to each other. Emily would not allow anyone to get close to her, except Laurie. It was sad to see how much Frannie loved Emily and how estranged mother and daughter were. Reeny admitted it was hard for anyone to love Emily. She pushed everyone away. It seemed as if Emily made herself unlovable. Sometimes Reeny thought the family loved Emily just because they had to. It was required that you love everyone in your family, no matter what they did. Blood is thicker than water was an old adage they all adhered to. Still, she wished Emily would come home for a visit. Emily should see Ben before he got any older and she missed out on his little boy years. Perhaps losing Stephen had hurt Emily much more that she allowed anyone to see. She would never open up and show her feelings, but Reeny knew it must have been hard on Emily when Stephen died. Stephen had loved Emily. They had their squabbles, as all siblings did, but sweet natured Stephen had never been mean or unkind to his little sister. Reeny had a feeling Emily was hurting more from Stephen's death than she admitted and that was partly why she stayed in Europe. Reeny's mind came back to the present and she made Laurie promise to follow up with her dad regarding those bruises. Frannie was due home in a few days and Reeny knew she would be worried if she saw Laurie with such ugly bruises on her arms.

Several days after her conversation with Laurie, Reeny drove to the airport to pick up her sister. Frannie rushed into Reeny's arms as she deplaned at LAX. She was so glad to be back in America. The flight from Paris was almost too much for a woman her age, but the trip had been worth it. After too many years of being estranged from her daughter, Frannie had taken the bull by the horns approach to their estrangement. Without any advance notice, she had purchased an airline ticket, made hotel reservations and had marched herself over to France to confront her daughter. Reeny could tell from the gleaming smile on Frannie's face it had been a good decision and a good trip. She ushered her flustered sister into the waiting car for the short ride back to Hollywood.

"She's in love, I can tell you that, Reeny," laughed Frannie, as she told her dear sister about her trip to Paris. They were sitting in Frannie's lovely home in the Hollywood Hills. Reeny glanced around at the photographs on the walls. There were so many pictures of Laurie as she was growing up. Reeny realized how much time Laurie had spent growing up in Frannie's home while she had been in sanatoriums. But those days were passed now. Her eyes took in the photograph of her handsome young nephew, Stephen, in his Army uniform. He looked so young. He still had blemishes on his face in the picture. Such a young age to die, too sad to dwell on. Next was her niece, that little gypsy girl Emily. She had grown into a famous artist. Pictures of Ben were the newest addition. Finally, her eyes landed on a very old photograph of her and Tom. It had been taken before he shipped out to Europe. Little did she know then he would return home to her a few short months later lying in a flag draped coffin. She and Frannie had suffered so much from mens' wars. She hated war. It was senseless and robbed wives, mothers, and sisters of their beloved men. God willing, she would not live to see any more wars. Frannie's exited voice brought her back to the present. "You would not believe she is the same girl. She is calm. She is focused. She is so very mature. She has grown up, Reeny. Finally she is a woman. She has found a place for herself in this world. I think for so many years she felt she was in Laurie and Stephen's shadows. Maybe I did that to her. I love Laurie so much and she needed me during those years you were sick. Emily was such a difficult child, I wanted to pretend she didn't exist. There was Laurie and Stephen, both such sweet natured children. Then there was Emily. It was like throwing a raging bee into the middle of two peaceful bunny rabbits." Frannie chuckled as she pictured her analogy in her mind. "Emily and I talked. I think we forgave each other for a lot of hurts unintentionally inflicted on each other. I love her so much, Reeny. Finally, we got close, like we have never been able to do before. I can say, at last, I feel like her mother. I love her like that. She isn't pushing me away. She's letting me love her, finally after twenty-five years she is letting me be her mother," Frannie said as her tears began to fall.

"Well, mop up your waterworks, you old lady, and tell me about Emily's new love," said Reeny, trying to get her sister back into a happier frame of mind. "Oh yes, Reeny, I nearly forgot. Emily is engaged to the most wonderful, handsome young Frenchman. His name is Jacque Vermillion. He is a journalist for the *Courrier International*. He comes from an old established French family. I met him and I can tell you he's very much in love with Emily. I can relax now. Emily is going to be just fine. She has a fabulous career and a great love. Philip is over the moon with happiness for her. He likes to take all the credit for how wonderful she turned out. He says it was his firm hand of discipline that kept her on the straight and narrow. What a crock! Emily was never on the straight and narrow. And the only firm hand Philip ever had was after his arthritis set in. But he's happy. Emily's happy and right now it seems like everyone is happy. Oh, Reeny, we are blessed. We've had our sorrows and our tragic losses, but we have held onto each other. I love you so much, Reeny. It's like you always tell me. We'll always be together. We have each other," said Frannie, as she went over and held her older sister in her arms. She loved Reeny so much. She could not imagine Reeny and her not being together. They were part of each other. Nothing would ever separate them while they were both still alive on this earth. The two middle-aged sisters sat in Frannie's home drinking tea until late into the evening. They were content with each other and with their memories.

CHAPTER 28

It was late when Reeny pulled into the garage of her home. There was a light still on in the living room. It was past midnight. Everyone should be in bed. Her heart fluttered. She immediately figured something was wrong with Ben. Perhaps he was sick. Quickly, she got out of the car and ran into the house. Brad was sitting on the couch. He was staring into an empty fireplace. Reeny did not like the heavy silence in the room. She had spent such a wonderful day in Hollywood with Frannie. She wanted to go back out the front door and drive back to Frannie's. She did not want her happiness to come to an end. Instinct told her the news would not be good.

"Sit down, Reeny," said Brad, as she walked into the living room. She set her purse down on the coffee table and sat on the sofa next to Brad. He took her hands into his own, rubbing them, as she noticed how cold his hands were. That was unusual. The house was warm. She should be the one with the cold hands having just come in from outside. She sat there looking at Brad who wasn't saying anything and her panic grew.

"What's the matter? What is wrong, Brad? Is it Ben? Is he sick?" asked Reeny frantically. Brad continued to rub her hands until the motion so infuriated her she grabbed them away from him and began hitting him on the chest with her closed fist demanding, "Tell me what's wrong. Don't make me suffer like this. Tell me now."

Brad looked right through his wife as if she wasn't even there as he said, "It's Laurie. She's sick, very sick. I got her test results back today. She has a disease called AIDS. There is very little known about it. It has just started showing up in hospital emergency rooms. It started showing up in homosexual men. Recently a link between the disease and intravenous drug use was discovered. I think it can be transmitted from a pregnant mother to her unborn child. We have to get Ben tested now too."

155

Laurie was only thirty-three years old and Ben had just turned six. They couldn't be too sick. They were too young. Reeny said calmly to Brad, "All right, we will take care of Laurie, get her well again. Does she need an operation? Does she need to go to the hospital? Is there an antibiotic we should have her start taking? You're the doctor, Brad. What do we need to do to make Laurie well again?"

The fatal disease referred to as acquired immune deficiency syndrome was a recent plague on the American people. Not much was known about it in the general public. But all that was soon to change. Cases were coming to the medical professionals' attention at an alarming rate and were increasing rapidly. Brad was not well versed in the details of the disease's migration to America. It was a specialized field and he was not an expert in it. He did know enough about the disease to make him very, very afraid for his daughter. He did not let his fear generate to Reeny. He did not want Reeny to know how scared he was for Laurie and Ben. They would do everything possible for Laurie. Somehow he would save his daughter. If he could not do it alone, he would call in all the favors anyone owed him. He had friends in every medical discipline. With their expertise he would save his daughter's life.

The immediate thing to do was to have Ben tested. Any disease the mother had could be transmitted to her fetus through her blood supply to her baby. That meant there was a possibility of this disease being transferred from a mother to her fetus in utero. Unlike Laurie, Ben showed no signs of being ill. Brad had studied information on AIDS and learned it was transmitted by blood borne pathogens, commonly through anal sex or the sharing of hypodermic syringes among intravenous drug users. Brad was fairly certain Laurie had been infected from sharing a syringe with someone already infected with the virus. How cruel God could be. His Laurie had suffered enough for her past mistakes. Was God going to make her pay with her life also? Was God going to make Ben pay for Laurie's mistakes? It was too horrible to even think about. Laurie had almost seven years of clean and sober living. She had turned her entire life around. She was getting her master's degree in education. She had a beautiful young son. This could not be happening to her. He wanted to go to Oregon and find that son of bitch who was Ben's father and tear him apart limb by limb for doing this to his baby girl. What kind of man would influence his girlfriend to start using drugs? Brad did not know he was capable of such hatred for another human being. His profession was to save lives, not want to end them.

During the coming months, Frannie and Reeny were forced to tap unknown resources of their strength. They leaned heavily on each other to walk their girl through her journey of fighting her debilitating illness. Many times they faltered. When one fell down, the other picked her up. They prayed, cried, and cursed the Lord. They could make no sense of what was happening to their beloved Laurie. She was their most precious treasure, yet they could not save her. She was the ribbon that tied them together. Through countless days, weeks, and hours, they stayed by her bedside, nursing her and each other.

"Mom, Mom, help me, I need the bucket again. The medicine is making me nauseous," rasped Laurie, as she leaned over her bed to throw up. Reeny rushed over with the plastic bucket they kept for Laurie to throw up in. It had been almost a year now since Laurie became ill. Sorrow had once again slithered into Frannie and Reeny's life in the most hideous way. Both sisters had been devastated upon learning the full extent of Laurie's illness. Laurie was "their" baby. If you wanted to blame God, you could say he smite them both down by striking at Laurie. That was one sure way to wound both sisters equally. To the family's surprise and relief, Reeny became the stronger of the two sisters. She, who for so many years had been unable to face life's ups and downs, was now the one who held her family together. She nursed her daughter. She propped up her sister and forced her to go on living for Laurie's sake. Rudely, she got into Frannie's face, demanding she get a grip on herself. She needed Frannie's help in this final segment of Laurie's life. She forcefully reminded Frannie the two of them had brought Laurie into this world and the two of them, together, would see her out of it. There was no time now to dwell on their sorrow. There would be time enough for that when Laurie was gone. Reeny was vigilant in her determination that Laurie would end her days peacefully, secure in the knowledge that her dear little son, Ben, would be well cared for by Reeny and Brad.

Frannie sat beside Laurie watching her sleep. It broke Frannie's heart to see the huge purple bruises on Laurie's face. The purple splotches were everywhere on Laurie's thin body. She was getting weaker everyday. Reeny was adamant Laurie would stay home as long as possible. Together, Frannie and Reeny nursed their daughter, this child whose true birthright they had kept secret for so many years. Only now, as Frannie sat there looking at her beloved daughter, did she regret her decision to deny her claim to her daughter. So many years ago, she had been so young and so much was going on. Reeny was so hurt from losing Tom and her own baby. Tim was going away to college. She was just a scared, confused kid herself. As she sat there knowing she was losing Laurie forever, she wondered if she had been wrong in not letting Tim know he had a daughter, especially one so wonderful as Laurie. But her initial decision to let Reeny become Laurie's mother had set everyone's life on a distinct course. Once that decision had been made, she could never tell anyone the truth about Laurie. Too many lives would be affected by that truth, especially Laurie's. No, she loved Laurie too much to ever tell her the truth. She never wanted Laurie to doubt how much she was loved. To tell Laurie the truth may ease Frannie's conscience, but it would only hurt Laurie. She might wonder why Frannie had done it. No, Laurie would leave this world secure in the knowledge that Reeny was her mother who loved her beyond life itself and Frannie was her aunt who also loved her.

Frannie woke from her doze when she heard Laurie moaning. She leaned down to Laurie's face and she heard Laurie say in a whisper, "Aunt Frannie, are you there? I can't see you, but I can smell you so I know you are next to me. Please, Aunt Frannie, hold my hands. They feel cold." Frannie took Laurie's hands in her own trying to warm them up as she moved onto the bed beside Laurie and laid down next to her. Laurie had grown so thin. The twin hospital bed easily held the two of them. Frannie cuddled Laurie up next too her. She held her in a fetal position, just as she had carried her in her womb over thirty-four years ago. Here was her beloved child, this darling woman. Laurie had brought so much happiness to so many people. Frannie remembered back when only sweet natured Laurie could love Emily. Laurie was the only person Emily had truly loved while she was growing up. Laurie was the only person Emily did not push away from her. Now Laurie was leaving them all. Frannie was desolate. How would they go on without Laurie in their lives? She was the sunshine in each day. She brought joy wherever she went. She had a little boy who needed her. Oh, God, why are you taking Laurie? We need her so much. Frannie had spent months cursing God, all to no avail. God was showing no mercy this time. It was obvious He wanted Laurie and He was taking her. All the medication in the world was not going to save Laurie.

Reeny had finally put her foot down and demanded that everyone quit being so selfish and start thinking about Laurie. She was the one dying. Everyone better put on a decent face and deal with it. Her daughter was not going to die amongst a bunch of depressed, emotionally distraught relatives. Reeny demanded that you put on an appropriately cheerful face and help Laurie leave this world with grace. If you couldn't do this then you got the hell away, and stayed away, until you could deal with Laurie's passing. She pointed out that even Ben was handling Laurie's eminent passing better than most of the adults in Laurie's life and he was only six years old. She also reminded everyone not to hate God too much as he had spared Ben. Brad had Ben tested immediately after getting the news about Laurie. Ben had not contracted the deadly disease from his mother while he was in her womb. If there was an optimistic point in this whole nightmare, the sheer mercy of Ben being spared was it. Frannie tried to be strong as Reeny demanded. She laid there on the bed with Laurie and fell asleep.

CHAPTER 29

Emily could feel the baby kicking inside her during the plane ride back to the states. It was the first time she had been home since she left after her high school graduation eight years ago. If she had been one for self-recrimination, she might have suffered a twinge of guilt over the reason preempting her return home. But now Emily took life as it came to her. For many years, as she was growing up, she fought against everything and everyone in her life. It had caused her great turmoil and pain that she worked for years in therapy to rid herself of. Her heart ached for her dying cousin. That was the reason she was on this airplane. She would not let Laurie leave this world without saying goodbye to her. Laurie had been the one person who had loved her unconditionally. Every other person in her life had strings attached to their love. Emily knew she was different from her relatives. She looked different than the other blondes and brunettes in her family. She resembled her father, but even he did not have the strong dark gypsy looks she had. She had his dark wavy hair but her's was more blue black than his. Her mother's silver blonde, fair coloring had done nothing to mute the strong dark looks of her father's genes. If her emerald eyes were not identical to her Aunt Reeny's, she would wonder if she was truly her mother's daughter. At least having inherited Aunt Reeny's beautiful emerald eyes gave her some genetic link to her mother's side of the family.

The plane was descending and the baby was kicking like crazy. It must be affected by airplane travel. Maybe the baby could feel the movement in utero more than she could feel it in her seat. She and Jacque had gotten married as soon as she learned she was pregnant. Jacque came from an old, aristocratic French family and any child of his must be truly legitimate. She thought he was rather old-fashioned about it, but she loved him and wanted to be his wife. Better they were married anyway. He was brutishly sexy and she couldn't keep her hands off him. Being pregnant only made her desire him more often. He wanted to come with her to the States, but she told him no. This was something she wanted to do alone. She was a very independent woman and she wanted to say goodbye to Laurie by herself. This was part of her life she did not want to share with her husband. He had never met her family, except for her mother, who had traveled to France a couple years ago before she got married. She still had issues to deal with regarding her family and right now was not the time to mix her two transcontinental lives together. Emily relaxed in her seat, dozing off, and dreaming of times she spent growing up with Laurie.

Emily's arrival was good for the whole family. Remembering Emily's hostility towards everyone during her youth made her family wary of her. It soon became apparent that Emily had grown up. Everyone had made mistakes. Everyone had suffered. Yet they were a family. Families stuck together, especially in times of sorrow and tragedy. They bonded together and welcomed Emily back into their arms. As a woman with past experiences and new feelings, she was ready to accept her family wholeheartedly. As a family they made a strong force for those they loved. They leaned on each other, drawing strength to get them through the hard times that lie ahead.

It was a good day for Laurie. She was able to sit up in her hospital bed, which Reeny had moved into the living room so Laurie could feel the cool fall breezes on her face coming in from the open french doors. The disease had taken Laurie's eyesight and she could not see the beautiful red and gold leaves on the trees outside. But she could hear the rustle of the falling leaves and the crackle of a stiff leaf hitting the driveway. As often happens, Laurie's hearing became more intense when she lost her sight. She cuddled Ben next to her. He was her precious boy. Somehow God had given her this wonderful child to love. God did not hold all her terrible mistakes against her. He had allowed her to have Ben. She was not angry that God was taking her away from Ben. She was only grateful that God was leaving Ben here so he could go on living the wonderful life she knew he would have. She did not know exactly where or when her own life had gone wrong. She had always tried to do the right thing. She had strived to make good grades, make her parents proud of her and lead a decent life. It was when she fell in love with Bennie that things had started to go so terribly wrong in her life. She had made some very bad choices and she was paying the price now. But she had made good choices also. One of the best choices she had made was having her son. She would only have him for a little while, but she knew her mom and Aunt Frannie would have him until they joined her in Heaven. She felt secure knowing she was leaving Ben in her mother and father's care. She knew she had wonderful parents. She just wished she had appreciated them more when she was younger and had listened to their advice. Now was not the time to beat herself up for her mistakes. She was finished doing that. She had spent hours with Ben telling him how much she loved him. In the early months of her sickness she and her mother had made tapes for Ben to listen to as he grew up. She and Reeny talked about her life growing up with Aunt Frannie and Stephen and Emily and Brad and Philip. Laurie tried to squeeze as many memories onto those Memorex tapes as she had strength for. It had been a healing time for her and her mother. They were able to forgive each other for any hurts, real or imagined. It was also her legacy to Ben. She wanted him to know his mother as he grew up.

Laurie drew on a renewed source of strength within her to get through those last days. She had been declining for a year, but as soon as Emily got there she seemed to recover much of her former strength and vibrancy. She had an increase in her energy level and in her appetite. She was able to keep down most of her food, which hadn't happened in months. These days were filled spending time with her family. She was not in pain so she did not have to take the narcotics that upset her stomach. She became the way she was before she got sick. Her eyesight was still gone and she was reed thin, but her exuberance with life was infectious. Ben was thrilled to see his mommy so vibrant and happy. She was able to get out of bed each day for a short while. Reeny and Ben pushed her around the house and out to the sun porch in her wheelchair. She and Emily were inseparable. They giggled and laughed for hours as Laurie held her hand on Emily's stomach feeling all the baby's movements.

"Em, take care of my mom and your mom for me, will you?" asked Laurie one evening as the two girls snuggled together in Laurie's bed. It was a tight fit with Emily's big stomach between them.

Never one to lie, Emily answered her cousin truthfully, "I'll do what I can, Laurie, but I won't lie and tell you I will be here with them. I have my life in Paris now. You know I have always been self-centered. I'm still selfish, but I'll promise you what I can. I'll stay in touch with them often. I'll call often and I'll come to the States when I can. Don't worry, Laurie. They have each other. It's always been the two of them. Even when Grandma and Grandpa McFadden died years ago, they clung to each other and wouldn't let anyone in the family help them. Those two ladies are tougher than they look. Ben's in good hands with them."

Sometime during the night Emily woke up to Laurie's moaning. Laurie was calling for Frannie. She seemed to be delirious. Emily lifted her huge stomach and rolled out of the hospital bed and went to get her mother. In Aunt Reeny's guest room both her parents were asleep in the double bed. She gently shook her mother, telling her Laurie wanted her. Together all three of them went back to the living room. Frannie crawled into bed with Laurie and cuddled her closely to her breast. Philip sat in the wingback chair by the french doors watching the stars twinkle in the dark winter sky. Emily went to the kitchen to put the teapot on the stove and then went upstairs to wake her Aunt Reeny and Uncle Brad.

Laurie and Frannie held each other close as Laurie said, "I love you, Aunt Frannie. You have always been my second mother. All those years you took care of me when Mom was sick I used to pretend you really were my mom. I felt bad about thinking that way because my own mom was sick and couldn't help it that she couldn't take care of me. Thank you for being my mom when she was sick. I'm lucky. I feel like I have always had two mothers. Frannie and Reeny, both my mothers. I am a very lucky woman to have been loved by two such wonderful mothers. Thank you, Aunt Frannie. I'll always love you."

As Frannie looked at her daughter's face, she saw tears fall from Laurie's lovely brown eyes. There was no sight in those pools of brown color, but they were deep with emotion and dreamy with thought. As Frannie held this daughter she had never been able to claim outright, her heart broke. Her child was leaving her now. It was not supposed to be this way. She had outlived two of her children. A mother was supposed to die first, not her children. It was too painful. Youth was able to handle pain better. The parent was supposed to die first. Stan and Stella and Aunt Lil and Uncle Herb had all passed away before any of their children. Frannie pushed her hurt away, cradling Laurie, crooning softly to her, telling her how much she loved her. She could feel and smell Reeny standing close to them. Yet she was wrapped in this cocoon with Laurie. Although the others were standing beside the bed, this warmth Frannie felt enveloped just her and Laurie. Together their souls touched as Laurie's soul left this earth.

Reeny let Frannie hold her daughter for a little while. She was unwilling to separate her from Laurie just yet. But Laurie was gone. Frannie must let her go. Reeny stroked her sister's head softly as she said, "She's gone, now Frannie. Please dear, you must get out of the bed. We have to make the call." Frannie started to remove Laurie's fingers from her own. Their fingers were entwined and lovingly Frannie untangled them. Her baby was gone now. She looked up at her older sister and faltered for a moment as she stepped onto the floor.

Brokenhearted, she said quietly so only Reeny could hear, "She's gone from us, Reeny. Our ribbon is gone. She kept us tied together in our love for her. What are we going to do without her?"

Reeny helped Frannie walk away from Laurie's bed as she answered her, "We have Ben to raise now. We promised Laurie we would raise him like she wanted us to. We must be sure that Ben never forgets his mother. He had an angel for a mother and now God has taken that angel home. We will raise him for Laurie. Come on, old gal, we still have a job ahead of us." Tears rolled down Reeny's face, slowing as they encountered the very fine lines of aging.

CHAPTER 30

Once again these two sisters stood together at a gravesite. Together, they were burying their child. Laurie was the woman whose birth had begun a secret they had shared for more than thirty-four years. Their child, who believed one sister was her mother and one sister was her aunt. Never once in her life did she suspect the two sisters had reversed their roles. She was gone now, leaving them at such a young age. Life had dealt a harsh hand to many young people of Laurie's generation. They became know as the baby boomer generation. With their inquisitive minds, combined with their loving hearts, they had created a vibration felt across an entire nation. They were a generation in motion, anxious to get places and get there fast. A war had waged in Vietnam, taking a multitude of young men from their generation. Another war, in the form of drugs, had ravaged Laurie and her peers right here on their own soil. Between the war in Vietnam and the damage caused by drug use, they paid a high price in their search of individualism and change. But they didn't give up. They righted the wrong mistakes they made and they learned from them. They admitted failure, but never defeat. Laurie's generation made tremendous changes in America. For these changes, many had paid the price with their lives. Hopefully future generations would appreciate the sacrifices their parents had made for them to be able to live in a more aware and tolerant world.

As Reeny and Frannie laid their precious Laurie to rest, they knew their secret would not die with Laurie. They still had been Ben, Laurie's precious son. As the secret continued to weave within their lives, Ben would be raised as Reeny's grandson, just as Laurie had been raised as Reeny's daughter. Once again, the sisters would share a child they both loved so much. With sad hearts and eyes focused on the future, Frannie and Reeny took hold of Ben's hands and lead him away from his mother's grave.

"Emily, you look so contented and happy. Thank you so much for coming at this difficult time. I know it was hard on you to travel so far in your advanced stage of this pregnancy," said Frannie to her lovely, plump daughter.

Emily replied, "Mom, nothing would have kept me away. I am happy. I'm in love with my husband. I have this new baby to look forward to. My only heartache is losing Laurie. Oh, Mom, why did God take her? She still had her son to raise. Laurie never hurt anyone. She was the kindest person who ever lived. Life is so unfair."

Frannie looked at her very pregnant daughter and could not bear to tell Emily how truly unfair life could be to people. Emily had so much to look forward to. Frannie silently asked God to protect Emily from life's cruelties.

Philip came in at that moment and said to them both, "Come on, my girls, it's time to get Emily on her plane back to Paris or she'll have that baby en route. It won't be much longer and the baby will be born and your mom and I will be coming over to see our first grandchild." For a quick second Frannie had a fleeting thought about Ben. Only she and Reeny knew that Ben was her first grandchild. Frannie quickly pushed that thought away. As always, Reeny held first place in that arena. Reeny was Ben's grandma and Frannie was Ben's great auntie. Frannie was having a grandchild, through Emily, that she could lay first claim to. She looked forward to the birth of Emily's child. She and Philip planned to go to Paris right after the baby arrived.

A month later as Frannie was getting some clothes cleaned and ready to pack on a moment's notice, she was surprised when Philip came home in the middle of the morning. She quickly moved the suitcases off the bed. She saw immediately that Philip was unwell. His color was ashen, he was quiet, and went straight to the bed to lie down. She pushed down the panic growing in the pit of her stomach. She went to get Philip the glass of cold water he asked her for. A few minutes later she returned with a cool glass of water and found Philip unconscious on the bed. She rushed to the phone and called for an ambulance, all the time trying to keep control of her own rapidly beating heart.

She was pacing the hospital waiting room floor when Reeny and Brad rushed up to her, both full of questions. She looked up at Brad and said, "He's had a heart attack. They are doing surgery now but there's no guarantees he will make it. Brad, he's too young to have a heart attack. He's not even sixty years old yet. He's just a little older than you and Reeny and you're both in good health."

At that moment the doctor walked out and came up to Frannie. Looking at her he said, "Mrs. Sommers, it's not good. He has slipped into a coma. You may want to contact your daughter. If she wants to see him, she may want to come now." Stunned, Frannie sank onto the cold plastic chair in the hospital waiting room. Reeny and Brad sat on both sides of her, trying to comfort her.

Frannie looked at Reeny. explaining, "Emily can't come now. She is due to give birth any day. I better call her right away. Oh. God, what awful news to give her at this time." Frannie gave way to racking sobs as Reeny held her close.

Five days later Frannie and Reeny stood silently together as they buried another member of their beloved family. Frannie stood there thinking she and Philip should be in Paris now with Emily and her new daughter. What cruel twist of fate had taken Philip from her too soon? She had called Emily from the hospital the night Philip had his heart attack. Emily wanted to come to her father's bedside immediately. Frannie thought it was the stress of Emily wanting to get back to the States and her helplessness in getting to her father before he died that pushed Emily into labor. It had been a long and very difficult birth, ending in a caesarean section. Frannie told Emily to stay in France and take care of herself and the baby. There was nothing Emily could do for her father. He was gone. Emily's baby was here. She must stay and take care of herself and her daughter. Frannie tried to assuage Emily's guilt over not being here for her dad's funeral. After many hours of transatlantic phone calls, Frannie finally convinced Emily to stay in France. She was healing from a difficult surgery and it would not do anyone any good if something were to happen to Emily. Frannie buried her husband alone. Of course many friends were there as well as Reeny, Brad, Ben, May and her daughters and their families. But basically, Frannie felt alone. Her son was gone, Laurie was gone, and Emily was in Europe. Just when she was feeling her deepest despair, she felt a hand on hers. She was brought back to the present by Ben's voice saying, "I love you, Aunt Frannie, don't cry. I'll be your little man. I'll grow up and take care of you. You'll always have me, Aunt Frannie." Somehow Ben's childish voice gave Frannie great comfort. For a moment she felt like Laurie was with her again. She squeezed Ben's hand and she knew she would be able to go on.

CHAPTER 31

For the next fifteen years Reeny and Frannie raised their beloved Ben. He was a constant source of joy to both these sisters as they approached their golden years. Being raised by grandparents, Ben had a wonderful sense of self and was more mature than other young adults. Ben loved his grandmother Reeny, his grandfather Brad and his great aunt Frannie with all his heart. He was devoted to his aging family and vowed always to care for them when they grew older. This was not to say Ben did not engage in all the normal ups and downs of growing up. He did. This was the second go around of parenting for each of these adults entrusted with Ben's care. Perhaps that helped them cope with Ben's childish antics. The ups and downs of parenting did not seem so traumatic the second time around. Between Reeny, Brad, and Frannie, they worked together getting Ben safely into manhood.

It was a different group that cheered for Ben as he walked across the stage to accept his high school diploma. His family consisted of grey haired ladies and a stooped gentleman. May's daughters' children, who were older than Ben, were about the youngest people in Ben's gathering of relatives. He was proud of his family. He knew he had a loving family. His grandparents and great aunt had taken over raising him after his mother had died when he was very young. He knew they were older, but he also knew they were much wiser than his friends' younger parents. They had kept him on the straight and narrow with their wisdom, guidance, and love. He felt blessed to have this wonderful aging family. He accepted his diploma proudly, winking at Grandma, Grandpa and Aunt Frannie.

Several weeks after Ben's graduation, the two aging ladies sat in Reeny's lovely sunlit breakfast nook having tea one morning. Frannie had long ago moved back to Pasadena to be near Reeny, Brad, and Ben. She had no ties in Hollywood with Phillip dead and

Emily in Europe. Emily's life was full of art shows and constant travel throughout the European continent with her husband and young daughter. For years Frannie wondered why Emily did not come to the States with her daughter. Frannie had only seen her granddaughter once when she was about a year old. Frannie had flown over to Paris to visit her daughter and meet her granddaughter. It had been a wonderful trip. Mother and daughter spent quality time together. Frannie was thrilled with her beautiful granddaughter. Emily had informed her mother she had no plans of ever returning to the States. Her life was in France now. Although she had dual citizenship, she considered France to be her home. Emily told Frannie there were too many sad memories for her back in the States. Frannie understood her daughter's feelings and reassured her young daughter it was permissible to feel that way. Frannie would not heap any guilt on Emily. Emily's childhood had been fraught with angry feelings over real and imagined hurts. Frannie felt it was time to put past demons to rest and accept her daughter any way she had to. If that meant having a transcontinental relationship, then so be it. Airplane travel was the mode of transit among this fast moving generation. Frannie felt she was a very "hip" granny and could walk the jet ways with the best of them. She had promised Emily she would return to France every so often to visit her and watch her granddaughter as she grew up.

Somehow the years had slipped by and Frannie had never returned to France. She and Emily stayed in touch by all the usual resources; phone, letters, pictures, and movie tapes. When the computer became all the rage, Frannie was thrilled with her e-mail connection to Emily. She received pictures of her growing granddaughter via e-mail at rapid speed. She could watch her granddaughter growing up with the help of her computer screen. For now Frannie pacified herself by keeping in touch by phone and computer. It was a sign of the times.

"Frannie, what are you thinking about? You haven't heard a word I've said. Sometimes I think you are getting senile," said Reeny, as she poured them each more tea. But Reeny was right. Frannie's mind did seem to wander back to the past more and more often.

Looking at Reeny, Frannie said, "Well then, what did you say?"

Reeny replied, "I was saying how strange life is. We've come full circle now with Ben going away to college." With just the two sisters in the room Reeny could be open. There was no need to keep their secret when it was just the two of them present. Reeny continued, "How strange that Ben is going to the same university that Tim went to all those years ago. Frannie, do you ever wonder how Tim is doing and how his life turned out? Do you ever regret not telling him about Laurie?"

Frannie looked over at this sister she loved so much and said, "Years ago when Laurie was so sick, I wanted to tell her the truth. I loved her so much and it was killing me, knowing she would die without ever knowing I was her real mother. But as I thought about it, I knew it was wrong to tell her. Her life had been lived with her believing certain things you and I had allowed her to believe. What good would it do to try to set her straight after all those years? I decided then it would only hurt her. I wanted her to die peacefully, knowing we both loved her so much. I think Laurie knew in her heart there was a special bond between the three of us. She never questioned it, she was just thankful for it. She told me once she felt like she had two mothers. And she did have two mothers, you and I. Then there was Ben to think about. Why change everything? No, Reeny, too much water has run under that bridge. It's too late for any regrets. We both did what we had to do at the time. It's all turned out fine. Ben is a wonderful young man. I'm sure Tim had a happy life. He was that kind of man. He was naturally good, kind, and gentle. I know he would not judge me on any of the choices I have made in my life. We've had enough of these sad thoughts. Let's be happy Ben is going away to Northwestern University. What a change from this warm state he has been raised in." The two sisters faced a new beginning for the grandchild they had raised.

Ben had been at Northwestern two years when his grandfather Brad passed away quietly in his sleep one night. He returned to Pasadena to help his grandmother with the funeral arrangements and to bury his grandfather who had raised him. He was young and strong and his grandmother and his Aunt Frannie leaned heavily on him. During this time in California he became aware that his beloved Grandmother and Great Aunt were getting older. With his grandfather gone, he began to worry about these two elderly ladies who loved each other so much and had never been parted their entire lives. Aunt Frannie's daughter lived in Europe and did not ever come to the States. Aunt Frannie was getting too old to make the trip to France anymore and hadn't seen Emily in over a decade. Emily made a quick trip by herself to attend her Uncle Brad's funeral but was anxious to get back to Europe to her husband and daughter. Ben thought his second cousin Emily a very cold person, but he supposed she had her reasons for her aloofness. He had never even met Emily's daughter but had heard she was a great beauty like her mother. But then, all the women in his family were beautiful. His grandmother and great aunt Frannie had been beautiful women in their youth and had passed their beauty down through the generations.

After his grandfather's funeral he met with his grandmother and great aunt. He knew they were both strong-willed women and he would have to do some very persuasive talking to get them to agree to his plans for their futures. He wanted to give these ladies plenty of time to consider what he had been thinking about since he returned to California to bury his grandfather.

"Please, Grandma, just think about it. I worry about you and Aunt Frannie being out here by yourselves. I love the Midwest and I plan on getting a job somewhere close to Northwestern University when I graduate. I have two more years to go so that gives you plenty of time to think about moving back where we can be close to each other," pleaded Ben. He glanced over at his still lovely but aging grandmother. She had raised him from the time he was a little boy. She had been his mother after his own precious mother had died so young. He did not like being so far away from her. She and Aunt Frannie had no one but him. His grandmother had some distant relatives from a first marriage, but he wasn't sure exactly what the connection was. They were descendants of her first husband's sister's children, but they did not come to visit very much and were scattered all over California. No, he would feel better having her and Aunt Frannie with him after he graduated in two years.

After visiting for several days with his grandma and great aunt it was time for Brad to return to school. The funeral was complete. Ben was reassured with his grandma's acceptance of her husband's passing. He returned to Northwestern University to complete the last two years of his program.

Several weeks after Ben left California Reeny had a small stroke that left her weak and confused at times. She was in her late sixties. She and Frannie lived together in her house in Pasadena. Frannie, being younger by six years, felt she could take care of Reeny after she came home from the hospital. However, Reeny seemed more confused as each day went by. The stroke had wiped out sections of her memory and Frannie spent hours trying to put the pieces back together. It was frustrating for both sisters. They had lived together for over sixty years, not always in the same house, but always close to each other. They shared a lifetime of memories. Now, only Frannie could string together their sixty years of memories. Day after day she repeated stories of long ago times and places. She identified the faces of loved ones Reeny could no longer remember. She told stories of bygone events. She related facts of family births and deaths over and over to Reeny to recapture some of her lost memories. Reeny might retain these memories for a day or two, but often she would wander up to Frannie with a picture of Laurie or Stephen and ask Frannie why they had this stranger's picture in their house. It hurt Frannie to the core of her heart to watch her beloved sister slipping away from her. Not in body, Reeny was still very robust, but her mind was getting old. Within a few months of Reeny returning home after her stroke, Frannie had to call Ben home to help make arrangements to move them both closer to him. She could no longer live alone and take care of Reeny.

Ben had hoped he would be graduated and settled somewhere himself before he had to move his grandmother and Aunt Frannie closer to him. But circumstances demanded he take a semester off from school and move his beloved grandma and her sister closer to him. Before he left for California, he drove down to Oak Creek, a small town south of the university. He remembered his grandma and Aunt Frannie had grown up in Oak Creek and thought it would be the perfect small town for them to settle down in during their retirement years. He could visit them often while he finished school. He found a wonderful assisted living facility who accepted both ladies. They would share a semi-private room. The living arrangements seemed perfect for these two elderly ladies in his life. He put a deposit down on their room, promising the administrator he would return soon with his grandmother and great aunt.

Ben took his temporary leave from school and traveled to California to take care of moving Reeny and Frannie. This was no small feat. These two ladies had combined two homes into one, at his grandma's house in Pasadena. The house in Pasadena was a sprawling ranch style home with over 2,500 square feet of space in the home. Two women and sixty years of living had filled the house to the brim. How was he going to explain to these ladies they could only take a minimum amount of belongings into their new living quarters? After a long evening with both his grandma and Aunt Frannie, he knew he was facing an impossible task. Grandma was what some people called "pleasantly confused" and Aunt Frannie was emotional. For a moment he got angry at his cousin Emily. She should be here helping her mother. But if he were truthful, he had to admit these ladies would not be separated. They had spent their entire lives together. Frannie would not go with Emily, even if Emily wanted her, which she did not. No, Reeny and Frannie would end their days together. This much Ben was sure of. So he buckled down to the task at hand. Feeling it was up to him to minimize the drama and make the decisions, he called in a professional to deal with the emotional trauma of reducing his beloved ladies memorabilia to saleable goods. He took his grandmother and Aunt Frannie on a week long vacation, explaining to them what was happening with their belongings and Reeny's home. He told each of them to pack five cardboard boxes with those items most important to each one. He felt so very cruel, asking these caring, little ladies to put their lifetime of memories into a minimum amount of cardboard boxes. As he watched their belongings accumulated throughout their lives reduced to a total of ten cardboard boxes, he vowed to keep his collectibles at a bare minimum his entire life. It was an excellent lesson that made him realize we all came to the same end. No one else wanted the physical, tangible byproducts of our memories. We came to the end of our lives and were reduced to what we could put in a few cardboard boxes. At least his Aunt Frannie still had her memories in her crystal clear mind, unlike his grandma who continued to suffer from increased dementia. He buckled down and did what he had to do to get his grandmother and great aunt back to the Midwest where he could look after them. He had found them a lovely place to live and he vowed to visit them often.

It took about a month to get everything sold and the finances of both ladies in order. Ben felt the ladies could handle driving back with him. He rented a nice, luxurious van, and planned a slow drive cross country. He wanted to spend some time with these two ladies who had raised him. He never took either of them for granted. He realized being raised by grandparents was a unique experience. Because of his own mother's death at a young age, he never forgot how quickly a person could lose someone they thought would be in their life forever. No, that's one thing he learned from a young age, never to take someone you loved for granted.

CHAPTER 32

With his precious ladies seat belted in the van, he checked the trailer lights. Making sure everything was hooked up properly, he hopped into the drivers seat. Fastening his seatbelt, he smiled and winked at his grandma who was riding in the passenger seat. Both ladies were so excited to be with the boy they had raised and loved so much. After long talks between the three of them, both ladies reassured him they did not mind disposing of their lifelong mementos. Much better to lose the material baggage of a lifetime and have the people you loved still near you. They both assured Ben the stuff could go, just as long as he stayed close to them. He reassured both his ladies how much he loved them and they never had to worry. He would be with them always. Even when he got married and had a family, they would still be his ladies, always in his life. Ben was never to forget that cross-country trek. During that time his grandma's dementia seemed to disappear. Her memory was crystal clear. The three of them shared a lifetime of memories. They talked about Ben's mother, memories he would forever cherish. They laughed as both ladies fought to talk about their girlhood to Ben. Frannie soon forgot her fear that Reeny might inadvertently reveal the secret of Laurie's birth because of her dementia. She was in perfect form. Her mind was clear. She was lucid and loved to tell Ben stories of his mother growing up between Pasadena and Hollywood. Ben knew the circumstances of his mother's death. He knew some of the background of his mother's life. He had always known who is biological father was but had never had any desire to look him up. His grandfather Brad had raised him and he was as good or better than any younger father could have been. Ben was happy with the people who had raised him. He preferred to enjoy his life and let sleeping dogs lie. Years later Ben looked back on this trip with his grandmother and great aunt as one of the most informative and rewarding times of his life. During this time he received a sense of peace and continuity of life that only these ladies who had loved him unconditionally his entire life could impart. He was forever grateful to them for this gift of their time, wisdom, and memories.

Ben graduated with honors. He was able to have his best ladies there for the ceremony. His grandmother and Aunt Frannie had settled comfortably into the retirement home. Grandma suffered from mild dementia, but the two sisters complimented one another perfectly. What Reeny forgot, Frannie filled in for her. They were able to carry on for many years like this. It baffled Ben that Emily never came to see her mother. He thought Emily's neglect of her mother was inexcusable. He bought Aunt Frannie a computer so she could keep in touch with Emily and her now grown granddaughter that she had only seen as a baby. Thank God for e-mail. That was the medium through which Frannie was able to watch her granddaughter grow up. Ben did admit Emily was great at e-mailing letters and photographs. She was a transcontinental e-mail specialist, but very selfish in Ben's opinion. His optimistic nature did not let him dwell on Emily's failure as the good daughter. Instead, he made sure he filled his grandma's and aunt's life as much as he could. He came often to visit them both, and when he could he took them on outings to interesting places he thought they would enjoy seeing. He was sad when he saw many of the elderly residents without visitors. On more than one occasion Ben thought how sad it was to grow old. He also thought how much sadder it is that young people do not appreciate the elderly relatives in their life. Perhaps the reason he had such a great appreciation of the elderly was because he was raised by his grandparents. He loved his grandma and great aunt and was thrilled they were able to attend his college graduation. Other than his cousin Emily in Europe, they were the only family he had left. Once again his graduation invitees consisted of these two grey haired ladies. With a pain in his heart, he felt the absence of his grandfather.

The next decade brought the expected decline in his grandmother and great aunt's mental and physical health. Frannie and Reeny had lived and slept side by side in their room at Oak Creek Assisted

Living Home for a dozen years. Their individual selves had meshed into a one pool of continuity. They were fluid together. They were always next to each other. They lived and moved in unison. What one started, the other finished. They were puzzle pieces fitted together. Ben felt it was only because of this predisposition for one to think and act for the other that had enabled the sisters to remain together for so long. He noticed several years ago his grandmother's mind was slipping away rapidly. He also noticed it was his aunt Frannie's protective covering up for her that kept the sisters together when in actuality Reeny should have left a couple years ago. It was obvious Reeny needed more care than the assisted living facility could give her. Frannie was fine, living here at Oak Creek. But she could not continue to care for Reeny. She was getting quite fragile herself. Ben knew he had the heartbreaking ordeal of having to separate these loving sisters.

In a way it was a blessing that Frannie's mind began to deteriorate about the same time Ben had to move his grandmother to a skilled nursing facility. Frannie was experiencing mild dementia and was not always aware that Reeny had moved out of the room they had shared for over twelve years. Almost every time Ben came to visit Aunt Frannie she asked when Reeny would be coming back. Ben did not have the heart to explain to Aunt Frannie that her sister would never be able to come back to their room. Reeny was in a nursing home and that is where she would stay until the end.

On a dark, cold winter day Ben parked his car in the parking lot of the retirement home. With a slow, defeated gait he entered the warm building and went looking for his Aunt Frannie. Ben saw her in the activities room of the home, talking with a nice looking elderly gentleman. It was good that Aunt Frannie was making friends. It would lessen the blow he had to deliver to her. He had just come from the nursing home where his grandmother had quietly passed away. In her eloquent way she simply left this world with no fuss. He was there at her bedside as she drifted away. He knew she went peacefully. She lay on the bed calmly, breathing shallowing and holding onto his hand. Her grip had relaxed on his hand and he heard her soft voice so he leaned over to hear what she was saying. His heart broke as he heard her call for her daughter, Laurie. He knew his grandmother had left this world and gone on to see his mother who had died at such a young age.

Now it was up to him to tell his Aunt Frannie that after more than 75 years she was in this world without her older sister. He could not recall a single day in his aunt's life that she had not been in contact with her sister. He tried desperately to think of a way to cushion the blow he must deal to this lovely old lady. Breathing a deep sigh and shaking his head, he resigned himself to the task he had to do.

"Hello, Ben, please meet my new friend, Mr. Slocum," said Frannie, as she glanced up at her great nephew. Immediately she saw the despair and sadness on Ben's face. Even in her mildly demented state of mind, she knew the worst had happened. She was alone. Her beloved older sister had left her. She looked over at Tim and knew he would never know the truth about Ben. No one would ever take her to see Reeny again. Reeny had left her. Reeny had gone to see Laurie and Stephen and Brad and Philip and Mom and Dad and Aunt Lil and Uncle Herb and all those people she had loved throughout her life. Here stood Ben with his anguished eyes focused on her. How like Tim he was. Sweet natured and kind beyond anything considered normal for a man. She loved this young man so dearly. In actuality, he was her's and Tim's grandson. But that did not matter anymore. He was a dear man, her nephew, and she loved him with all her heart. She could not help that Tim did not know Ben. Life had dealt her too many twists and turns to ever set the record straight. She pushed herself up onto her walker and laid her grey head on Ben's chest, comforting him. "It's alright, Ben. It was her time to go. I can wait awhile until I see her. I have you," Frannie said softly to Ben.

Politely, Ben acknowledged the elderly gentleman Aunt Frannie introduced him too. He seemed like a nice man. Tim Slocum was his name. Their eyes met for just a moment. Something about the man reminded Ben of his mother. He had that same aura his mother had. They had a calm, contented mannerism about themselves. For just a moment he thought how strange the similarity was. Shaking his head and chastising himself for his emotional meandering, he put his arms around Aunt Frannie and led her back to her bedroom.

Frannie was dressing for Reeny's funeral. She was confused. She did not know exactly when Reeny had died. Sometimes she totally forgot Reeny was dead and she absentmindedly asked staff where her sister was. When she asked people where her sister was they looked pityingly at her. She learned not to ask too often. The question stayed pushed to the back of her mind. Once in awhile it came to the forefront and she could not help but ask, "Where is my sister?" But right now she knew she was supposed to get dressed nicely. Ben was picking her up shortly. She heard a soft knocking on her door and turned, expecting to see Ben.

Her breath stopped in her chest and her heart fluttered dangerously. There in the doorway stood Reeny. Only Reeny was very young and beautiful, with her wavy auburn hair and her sparkling emerald eyes. Even her translucent skin was young and creamy again. As Frannie blinked her aging eyes, Emily stepped from behind the young, beautiful Reeny.

"Oh, Mother, I am so sorry. I have left you for far too long. And now Reeny is gone from us." Emily gathered this small, bent and greying mother of hers into her arms.

The beautiful girl, who looked exactly like Reeny when she was young, came up to Frannie and said, "Hello, Grandmere. You don't remember me. I've grown up. Try to remember me when I was a baby, Grandmere. It is me, Renae. Remember, I'm named after your beautiful sister, Reeny. I'm sorry, Grandmere, that your sister is gone." Renae spoke to her grandmother with a decidedly French accent.

Emily could see her mother was startled and could not comprehend the whole situation. Walking over to her mother, she gently took her arm and led her to a chair to sit down.

Ben walked into the room and saw the three women sitting in the far corner. Like Frannie, his breath was taken away when he saw Renae. She looked exactly like photos he had seen of his grandmother when she was young. The resemblance was startling.

As he walked up to his Aunt Frannie, she gazed lovingly up at him as she said, "Ben, my Emily has come home to me. And, Ben, I don't have to ask where Reeny is anymore. Emily has brought her back to me. I don't have to ask where my sister is. I know where she is now.

Ben glanced at Emily as they both looked at Renae. Yes, in a way Reeny had returned to them all.

THE END

Printed in the United States
28231LVS00001B/442-444

9 781413 748567